BUSY AIN'T
THE HALF OF IT

By Frederick Smith and Chaz Lamar Cruz

In Case You Forgot

Busy Ain't the Half of It

By Frederick Smith

Down For Whatever

Right Side of the Wrong Bed

Play It Forward

Visit us at www.boldstrokesbooks.com

BUSY AIN'T THE HALF OF IT

by

Frederick Smith
and Chaz Lamar Cruz

2021

BUSY AIN'T THE HALF OF IT

ISBN 13: 978-1-63555-944-6

This Trade Paperback Original Is Published By
Bold Strokes Books, Inc.
P.O. Box 249
Valley Falls, NY 12185

First Edition: August 2021

Credits
Editors: Jerry L. Wheeler and Stacia Seaman
Production Design: Stacia Seaman
Cover Design: Tammy Seidick

Acknowledgments

When we wrote our first novel together—*In Case You Forgot*—
we didn't know the amount of love and support we'd receive
from so many people. To all of the book clubs, podcasts,
professional and community organizations, book reviewers,
and readers—THANK YOU!

To our friends and family, even those who aren't readers, thank
you for the encouragement and support.

To the Black queer family, we are encouraged and excited to
be a part of the legacy of sharing our stories in our own way.

"If I love you, I love you. And if I love you and duck it, I die."
—James Baldwin talking to Maya Angelou (*Assignment America*, episode 119; "Conversation with a Native Son," May 13, 1975, Thirteen WNET)

THE PEOPLE

Elijah
Justin
Zaire
Justice
Junior
Lenay
Ezra
Jabari
Linda
Brenda
Aunt Vick
Uncle Ro
Trevor
Jeanine
Ke'Von
Sonoma
Jordan

CHAPTER ONE

Elijah: The Right Time

We're sitting at one of our favorite places to come to after a long night out—Kitchen 24, on Santa Monica Boulevard in West Hollywood.

I'm having a nightcap. My best friends, Ezra and Lenay, are both having tequila with their pancakes and bacon. Typically, if we are at Kitchen 24, it's because we're having a light dinner and drink in the early evening. I try not to stay out late like this because of my early morning routine and work. But today is not like our usual.

Tonight we are celebrating Ezra's return to center stage. They've been on a little sabbatical from drag performing, doing some experimenting with live singing to give themself a chance at becoming a solo singer. But tonight Micky's, one of the more popular clubs in West Hollywood, has welcomed Ezra, aka Chaztity Beltz, back with open arms and big tips.

First thing tomorrow morning, I'm scheduled to go to the farmers market with my Uncle Justin. Wish I could cancel because I already know sunglasses, aspirin, and water will be my only saving grace. The only thing keeping me from canceling is the fact that he hates when people change plans, so I'll suck it up and deal with the consequences of partying like I'm twenty-three. I'll have him pick me up from my boyfriend's apartment because I'm not in the mood to catch a Lyft to my home in K-town, not being this intoxicated. I'm a lightweight when it comes to drinking. I'm on my third and final drink. So, after this I'll feel more comfortable stumbling over to Zaire's. Which reminds me, let me text Uncle J, giving him that pickup update, and then call Zaire and ask if it's cool if I come crash at his place.

"I'm buzzin' it, y'all," I say as I start to get up from the table. "Let me call Zaire and ask if I could stay the night."

"You still ask?" Lenay says. "Y'all have been together too long for that. Can't you just text and say you're coming over?"

"Or just pop up unannounced," Ezra adds. "You know he wouldn't mind."

"I could," I say to Ezra. "I still like to ask. I don't like making assumptions. You both should know that."

I get up and head to the front of the restaurant for a little privacy from Ezra and Lenay.

"OMG, Chaztity Beltz is here!" I hear a group of young drag fans yell giddily as I walk out the front door to the sidewalk. They've spotted Ezra. I hope that makes them happy.

I haven't seen Zaire in four long days, as both of our work weeks have been busy. And although it's pushing two in the morning, I hope he answers because I'd like to hear his voice. Besides, I'm sure he's not asleep because we rarely go to bed without saying good night over the phone or text. It's a practice we've had since before our relationship became public and official two years ago. When the phone rings, there's a soft tickle in the pit of my stomach. It's only been four days without seeing each other, but I miss him. When did I become this smitten?

He picks up on the first ring.

"Hey, love," Zaire says. His voice is warm and raspy.

"Hi. Did I wake you?" I'm smiling.

Zaire asks me about my night and Chaztity Beltz's performance. I tell him I'm enjoying my night with Ezra and Lenay. I ask him about his night. He tells me he went over to see his nibling and came back home, ordered takeout, then Netflixed and chilled. I smile even more. He tells me he misses me. I ask him if I could come over after I finish eating. He tells me I never have to ask, and reminds me that's what the key he gave me is for. I feel warm and a bit misty eyed. I think I'm so gushy because I'm tipsy. Or maybe I really do just love him so damn much. I thank him and tell him I'll text him when I'm on my way so he can open the door.

"Use your key."

"I left it at home." I know this will be a slight annoyance. I honestly forgot that I had a key to his place. I never carry that key.

"You'll have to figure out how to get in, then," Zaire says. "Just kidding. Call me when you get here. See you soon, love."

When we hang up with each other, I turn to face the restaurant, which now has a long line. I guess Kitchen 24 is the place to be for everybody. It's nice to see more shades of brown skin in line now. Earlier, we were the only table of shades of brown.

Having a brief conversation with Zaire has me walking on bliss back to my table. But before I can sit myself down and readjust in the booth, Lenay asks, "Why aren't y'all living together, again?"

I continue to scoot myself into the center of my side of the table so I am sitting directly in the middle facing them both.

"That seems to be the question of the season," I say as I process my thoughts.

"Well, what's the answer of the season, darling?" Ezra says.

The truth is, it doesn't feel like the right time for us to

move in with each other, I think. But apparently that wasn't an inside thought, because Lenay says, "Well, when do you think the right time will be?"

"I don't know," I say and take another sip of my drink. "But I know he wants us to move in with each other."

"That's obvious," Lenay slurs. She's been drinking all night. She's on her second drink at Kitchen 24, and I know she had a few at Ezra's performance earlier.

Zaire and I have been together for two years. He lives here in West Hollywood. I live in Koreatown. They're not that far from each other, around six Los Angeles miles. Which is nothing. Hauling our things to and fro is a custom I've accepted, but for Zaire it's an unnecessary inconvenience he despises. He feels it would be easier for me to move in with him. I'm comfortable having my own apartment, having one housemate who isn't home often, having my own bathroom, having a place I can go to that's mine.

I've never lived with a partner, and it isn't something I daydream about. I'm open to the idea, but I prefer the idea of living by myself, being without a housemate, to see how that feels first. I want to know that feeling. Zaire has had a different experience. He's been in a long-term relationship, he's been married. He's lived with his ex-spouse. And as of last year, he lives alone. His roommate moved out last year to return to the East Coast. Zaire took over the lease. He didn't want or need a housemate. So he lives in a two-bedroom, one-bathroom flat, here in the heart of gay L.A.—WeHo.

Where Zaire is more open to sharing and balancing space and time with many people—he's the eldest of four and a divorcée—I am more reserved. I'm an only child, and this relationship is the first to last longer than four months. I haven't needed to share or balance negotiating space and time with many people. My friends, Ezra and Lenay, have been helpful and teaching me the value of partnership and sharing. I'm grateful for them for that.

"I want to experience living alone first before I move in with a partner," I tell them. I'm coming from a vulnerable place. There is silence, and for a moment I think this would be enough of a reason for the conversation to evolve into another topic.

"But you already live on your own," Ezra states as if they're being cautious of saying something that may hurt my feelings. That's rather bizarre, considering they're usually brash with providing me feedback.

"I still have a housemate. I want to know what it feels like to actually *live alone*," I say, *un peu* pointed.

"But you kinda do already," Ezra says.

"I still have a housemate, Ezra," I say as I feel my heart-beat speeding up. "I want to live by myself before I move in with a partner. Is that bad?"

The server comes and asks if she could take a picture with Chaztity Beltz before we leave and if we need another round of anything.

"Of course!" Chaztity Beltz, aka Ezra, says.

"I'll have another round," Lenay says.

"No, she's good. We're good. We can have more water please, darlin?" Chaztity Beltz chimes in.

Lenay looks at Ezra and laughs. "You're right. I really don't need another drink."

I am quiet. There's a lull in conversation until the server returns with our waters.

Ezra then starts humming a tune that sounds pretty good. Lenay harmonizes with Ezra, then stops and looks at me. "Does Zaire know about you and Jordan?"

Random.

Ezra stops mid singing to say "LAH-NAY!" in a melodramatic drag cadence. When Ezra is in Chaztity Beltz drag, their persona comes out every now and then. Well, it never really goes away. It helps for comedic relief at times. This isn't one of those times.

I look at Lenay, slightly confused.

"What do you mean, know about me and Jordan? What's there for him to know?" I say, perhaps a bit more defensive than I need.

"Didn't y'all have sex a few times?"

Jordan is Zaire's best friend. We had sex twice. The first time was a few springs ago, and the second and last time was a little over two years ago, right before my first date with Zaire.

"We did have sex." I take a sip of water. "Twice, to be exact. But that was before Zaire and I…"

Then there is that uncomfortable silence, as I pause talking and reflect on what I'm saying. No one is making eye contact with me. This is weird.

"What does that have to do with living together?" I break the silence.

"Well, aren't you always talking about the unconscious thoughts at times impacting our actions?" Lenay says. "What if you're holding on to the fact that you haven't shared that you and his best friend had sex before?"

I hadn't thought about that before. I'm not sold on the idea that I don't want to move in with Zaire because I've had sex with his best friend before I even knew he existed. But Lenay has some merit. I haven't told Zaire, but it's been two years. How do I tell him this secret I've held so long into our relationship? Why would I do that? When?

"But who knows. I could be wrong," Lenay says. "Don't take any relationship advice from me. My remedy for any issue is to just break up." She's mostly telling the truth. She's a serial dater. No one makes it past two months.

Then the server comes with our check and tells us the guy at the entrance paid for the bill.

I turn to look toward the door and there stands Zaire in his nighttime workout gear of short running shorts, long socks, and an oversized T-shirt.

"I hadn't thought about that before, Lenay," I say as I get up from the table. "I'd love to hear your thoughts too, Ezra. Let's talk about it later."

I leave my best friends oohing and ahhing over Zaire's gesture and surprise visit. When I reach Zaire, I fall into his open arms for a beautiful hug. I kiss his neck.

"Such a nice surprise. And right on time," I say as we walk out. "Let's go home."

"Shall we?" Zaire opens the door for me.

CHAPTER TWO

Justin: The Timing Is Off

It's a little after midnight, and since it's the weekend and since it's my house and since my young ones are out at a summer dance at their high school, I've decided a third glass of wine with Trevor is all right tonight. I'm relaxed and a little bit buzzed, but enjoying the mood and the moment. The fire pit, the full moon, and the slight breeze make this a perfect friend-date night.

I rarely have the house to myself on weekends. Justice and Junior, my sixteen-year-old fraternal twins, are usually home from their boarding school in Burbank on weekends and also during summer break, unless their cousin Elijah decides to drive them around L.A. on their little dates and friend outings. Or unless they get in a mood and decide to stay in their residence hall for the weekend. And it's rare for Trevor, my best friend, to be in on a weekend night. He's usually out on a date, a hookup, or some kind of adventure with a new man.

"You sure you can handle this, Justin?" He does another heavy pour into my glass. We've just opened up a second bottle of a Corner 103 Pinot Noir that Trevor picked up a few weeks ago when he took a date on a weekend trip to the Sonoma Valley. "I don't need you getting too tipsy on me tonight."

"Not like either of us gotta drive anywhere." We clink glasses again. We always toast with every new drink we start. Have for as long as we've known each other. Trevor is my most genuine friend in L.A., where everyone seems to have an agenda, in my opinion, and I love that we don't talk shop when we're together. "All I gotta do is go inside and walk down the hallway—and you, a quick stumble through the backyard next door."

"I wish I was stumbling into somebody's bed tonight," Trevor says, picking up his phone with his spare hand. Probably scrolling the apps with his made-up avatar so no one recognizes him for who he really is. "You wanna help me with that?"

"Help you with what?"

"Never mind, Justin," he says. "Let's just finish this last bottle so I can get Sonoma out of my head. That's what I get trying to date someone 'regular.' And don't say anything. I know I date 'regular.' I date 'celebrity' too, with that one app for public figures to find each other, but that feels too staged."

Trevor air quotes *regular* and *celebrity*.

I know what he means, and I know it's not being judgmental, given our status in life. I wish I had the same courage Trevor has when it comes to dating people who aren't as well-known as we are. Hell, I wish I had the courage to *date*. It's been three years since my ex-wife, Jeanine, left to find her bliss, but dating and finding bliss are not things I really have the time to do at this point in my life.

I anchor the weekday *More at Four with Justin Monroe* and co-anchor the *Live at Five L.A.* newscasts. Trevor— Trevor Smith to everyone else—does the four and five o'clock newscasts at a rival station across town. We're making history in Los Angeles, being Black men and being the main anchors L.A. turns to for news and information. I've been number one in the ratings for over sixteen years, and Trevor's newscasts are a close number two. Still, leading our field and the L.A. airwaves is a surprise, given the amount of disdain for journalists—let alone Black journalists—by trolls who hide behind anonymous identities. Fake news, some of the people on the extreme right call what Trevor and I do. I call it seeking the truth. I've also gotten called the f-word, n-word, and n-f words more than I've ever been called in my professional career.

Same for Trevor. Which is why we click as we do. We get each other.

In addition to being a professional colleague and rival, Trevor also is my next-door neighbor and one of my best friends since our undergraduate journalism school days. We've known each other before we were *the* Justin Monroe and *the* Trevor Smith. Our familiarity with each other triumphs over any news story, anchor desk, or rivalry that would come between us and our twenty-plus-year friendship.

"But you always date 'regular,' and I don't know why or how you do it," I say and sip. "Don't you get nervous about stalkers, people who like you because of what you represent being on TV, or those who are trying to get close to your money?"

"I guess I'm not as cautious as you. But I get it. You got obligations, kids, family, your reputation, and respectability."

"Not necessarily reputation or respectability," I say. "I'm not trying to be one of those forty-something down-low men afraid to be myself. That's so nineties. I just don't have the time to date. Maybe when the young ones go off to college in a year or so."

"Well, in the meantime, I'm not trying to have someone fill out a five-page non-disclosure clause just to date or fuck," Trevor says and fills up his empty wine glass. "And in case you forgot, Black may not crack, but we're not getting any younger."

I want to say something like, *and you're number two in the ratings because you put men and dating above everything else,* but instead, I say, "You sound like my nephew, Elijah. Always trying to get me to loosen up and throw caution to the wind."

"You wanna fix it for me, Justin?"

"Fix what?"

"This." He stands up from the patio chair, gesturing his hands up and down his body before sitting down again. "I mean my dating life. Give me something to settle down for?"

"Oh, that."

I love and hate that Trevor flirts like this when we're drinking. Even when we're not drinking. I don't think the flirting is in my head either, and I don't think he's really conscious of it. Trevor is, and has always been, a charming and flirtatious person ever since we were undergrads in the Mizzou School of Journalism. I take a long sip of the Pinot.

"Yeah, this."

"Well, I don't know what to say about your dating life or settling down."

"You usually have something to say about everything, Justin," Trevor says. "But whatever."

"Whatever back. Besides, what do I know? I did the settling down thing once, and she left to be a free woman. And I'm happy we can now both be free to be who we are."

"It's a blessing in disguise." Trevor chuckles. "Because you were both performing something you never really felt— straight life, marriage, two kids, white picket fence, trying to be a modern-day Banks family from *Fresh Prince*, but in Ladera Heights instead of Bel-Air."

"You should be a therapist instead of a journalist."

"I knew you were gay from the first time we met back in Mark Twain Hall," Trevor says. "And I am not saying or buying that 'I'm bi' transition thing."

"But I am. Bi. Fluid. Open. Down for whatever. Single."

"Whatever you say, best friend. I'm just glad you and Jeanine ended things on good terms."

"I still pay alimony, which I don't mind doing," I say. "But I have Jus and Junior, so that more than makes up for anything I owe Jeanine."

"Hmm. Hey, maybe you can capitalize on your platform as L.A.'s number one anchor and turn your story into a reality show." He lights up even more as he's talking.

"Nope."

"And put your gay nephew, Elijah, on it, too. Might kick-start his acting career, finally. And of course me, your TV competition and bestie, as the slutty comic sidekick."

"Tell me how you really feel, Trev."

My phone buzzes. Thank goodness. No way I'm putting my life and my young ones through the drama of a reality show. Speaking of which, there's a text from the twins. The school dance is over, and they're waiting for the driver I hired to bring them back home tonight, though they could have just stayed in the campus residence halls if they wanted. Elijah, who I'd usually pay to drive them around for me, is on date night or friend's night out or something like that.

"Jus and Junior are on their way home soon," I say.

"That's another reason you need to get back out there. Your young ones, as you like to call them, will be out the house and off to college in another year."

"Don't say that. I'm not ready."

"Like I said, we're in our forties and definitely not getting any younger unless you or I lie on that table." Trevor pulls his face back to simulate getting a facelift. "Anyway, who am I but someone who's known and loved you for like ever."

Ugh. He can't love me.

I think Trevor knows I've had a thing for him since we were nineteen-year-old undergrads, since before I got involved with my ex-wife Jeanine, since before I had the twins and the life I have now as a single parent and a journalist. If he doesn't know, then he's clueless. Whether he knows it or not, I've had a thing for him since the day we met at a residence hall council meeting over twenty-five years ago.

Truth be told, I wish I was his lover. Or, at minimum, that we had an arrangement. I could be like one of his apps hookups and dates, but one who he actually knows, loves, and respects. Maybe even a friends-with-benefits deal for people like us who are in *the industry* and can't exactly head to the mall or a club or out on the streets and find someone to date.

I'm often finding myself happily jealous Trevor has found the courage and freedom to be himself fully and not be nervous dating whomever he wants. It's the same freedom I supported my ex-wife, Jeanine, to seek when she said that with everything bad happening in the world in these times, she needed to go out, leave the young ones and me, seek her joy, and be a free Black woman.

I thought this crush on Trevor would end in my twenties and not be a part of life in my forties. But here I am, single, happy, envious of Trevor's life, and wanting to be something other than the best friend pining for more.

Project List

- Find out if undergrad and grad schools have awarded the scholarship funds I've donated. If not, why?—Alumni Association(s)
- Schedule colonoscopy. Keep it personal or use it for on-air story about Black men's health?—personal
- Is the Ojai place underutilized? Do we need it?—Felicia
- Why is the roof on parents' house leaking after only two years?—Deandre/Uncle Ro
- Are taxes paid and up-to-date?—Felicia
- Find a new trainer and gym equipment—Elijah
- Jus & Junior orthodontics follow-up—Elijah
- Change esthetician and related work—ask Trevor for recommendation
- Check in on former intern Ke'Von—personal
- Voting rights and voter suppression; potential story—personal, follow-up with contacts
- Is lease up on car(s)?—Felicia
- Check in on Louisiana and Sacramento family finances—personal; maybe Brenda
- Increase monthly to In The Meantime organization—Felicia
- Birth control issues for Justin and Justice—personal, Elijah, Jeanine
- ~~Time for a winter vacation?~~
- Contacts for Elijah's acting work—personal; contacts
- Added security to house; for Justin and Justice—personal, Felicia
- Review contract renewal—Felicia

Chapter Three

Justin: Live At Five

"Uncle J, I know you're ignoring me," I hear through the car speakers. It's my favorite nephew, Elijah. My only nephew. I've given him the security code to my retreat house property in Ojai so he can *center* himself, as he calls it, while he prepares for yet another audition and role he probably won't get. I'm not a dream killer to the young ones in my family, but Elijah is almost thirty—maybe just over thirty—and has not yet been discovered by Hollywood or the Broadway stage. And I have plenty of contacts who could make Elijah's career take off if he would just let me. Yet he wants to know, "You going to Miami with us or not?"

I knew I should have kept my big mouth shut about having a two-week break from parenting and work coming up. Brenda, my oldest sister and Elijah's mom, can't manage information for anything. But I had to let her know the twins changed their mind about visiting her and our side of the family in Sacramento, so they could see their mom's family instead. I'm sure that didn't sit over well with Brenda, but that's another story that partially explains why Elijah came to L.A. to live close to me.

The busy-ness of family drama.

I have just dropped off my twins, Justice and Justin Jr., at LAX.

Hallelujah.

I am looking forward to a mini-reprieve from parenting two sixteen-year-olds for a bit. I have a lot to do, and a whole lot of nothing to do, if that makes sense, while my young ones are gone.

Instead of going to Sacramento to see their Aunt Brenda and my parents, Jus and Junior decided at the last minute to spend the remaining two weeks of summer break with their mother's parents, who have promised them a good time in Brooklyn. They've also promised visits to a few of the historically Black colleges and universities that they, as Black academics, have connections to on the East Coast. I can't blame Jus and Junior for wanting to forgo Brenda or the summer trips to some of the West Coast private campuses their academy has planned.

The forty grand each I pay for their yearly tuition and room and board provides my young ones with a stellar education, small classes, lots of attention, access to resources, and connections with people I never had growing up. However, when it comes to feeding and affirming their Blackness, the academy falls flat. I know it. Jus and Junior know it, too. And I'll be letting the academy know it when I pop up at parent-teacher conferences in a couple days.

"I'm driving," I remind Elijah as I speak to the air microphone somewhere in my SUV. "You know how I get trying to navigate and talk at the same time. How's Ojai?"

Call me a boomer. Well, my young ones call me that when I don't handle technology and other tasks simultaneously. Like driving and speakerphone conversations.

I know my nephew's heart and concern for me are in the right place, just like Trevor's. Elijah's queer. I'm fluid, as my young ones say. I need to explore my sexuality. They've also given me permission to get back out there and date, since it's been three years since their mom and I divorced. And now that I'm no longer married, I am ready to think about finding time to put myself out there, I think—no, I know—with a man, this time around. I'm open.

"Ojai is nice. Per usual. Thanks for letting me have it this weekend, Uncle J," Elijah says. "Sorry to put pressure on you. If that's what it feels like."

"Please." I decide spontaneously to turn on LaBrea. I am going to work on my day off. "You can't pressure me, Elijah. I keep you afloat. And your mama. And your cousins. And many of the Monroes up in Sacramento and down in Louisiana, too."

"That's ego, Uncle J," Elijah says. "Your vibration is messing up my energy."

"Sorry, Elijah." Sometimes I feel like I've got so much on my plate with my family and the extended family that I can sometimes say out loud what's in my head instead of shutting up. I don't say this to Elijah, though. "It is. I didn't mean that. I told you, I'm driving."

"All good," Elijah says. "I'm just looking out. My crew likes you and said it's okay for me to invite my famous uncle. They're discreet and background checked, if you're worried about it. You can bring your bestie, Trevor, if you want."

"Not worried about your friends, but probably not going to Miami, though. I'll let you know when I let you know. And Trevor's working. I'm the one taking time off."

"Bet. I'll link up, then, when I'm closing up Ojai and on the way back to L.A."

"Enjoy. Get centered. Good luck on the audition prep, too."

"Thanks, Uncle J, I appreciate that," Elijah says. "Can I run something by you quickly?"

"Any time. What's on your mind?"

"I'm not just here for the audition, though I am hoping this one is my big break. I needed a short break from Zaire. He kinda insisted he should come to Ojai with me, but I didn't give in. And there was no drama. Ashe."

That makes me sad to hear something is up with Elijah and Zaire. Of all the guys Elijah has brought home, so to speak, Zaire is my favorite. He's kind. He loves his family. He's in a career that he wants to do and that he loves. Definitely the one who brings the most to the table with Elijah. I'm a father and an uncle. I'm protective. And concerned.

"Are you and Zaire fighting or having problems?"

"You know what?" Elijah says. "Never mind. I'm just getting centered for my audition."

"Nice. Enjoy your 'get centered for another audition' weekend. Or whatever you're calling it. I know when you're not being fully truthful about your feelings."

"Don't be like that now, Uncle J, but thank youuuuu," Elijah says. "Just keep me posted if you wanna go."

"I'm busy. In fact, I'm pulling into the station now. Someone has to float all of y'all."

"Thank you, Uncle."

"Eat and drink all you want," I say. "Go get a spa treatment while you're in Ojai. Talk later."

"Love you, Uncle J."

"Love you, Elijah."

Since I'm hardly at the station on weekends, I don't recognize security at the front drive-through gate. Of course, the guard knows me—I'm Justin Monroe, after all—and lets the gates open with barely a flash of my station ID, and none of the small talk that the weekday crew likes to make with me. A few yards into the station compound, I notice a car I don't recognize is parked in my spot. I make a mental note, park in a visitor spot a few spaces away, grab my work bag, and head into the station.

"Whose car is in my spot?" I ask the front desk receptionist, more rhetorically than really wanting to know. It's not a big deal, but I do want it noted that it's *my* spot. It's been earned, and I know that question will make its way through the staff so that there are no more mistakes like that.

I breeze down the hallway to where the on-air talent offices are. The lights are on in the studio, and I hear the chatter of some of the directors, producers, our news director, and others. It's barely noon. We don't do a noon newscast on Saturdays. I stand outside the studio.

"…this time, with a little more friendly authority in your voice…"

"Good afternoon, L.A. Welcome to *More at Four*. I'm Ke'Von Carrington. Here are today's headlines."

Wait? Ke'Von, the Mizzou journalism student who interned with us at the station four summers ago? Who I sponsored for his first NABJ conference? Who needed a new wardrobe and thousands of dollars of dental work that I put in his graduation GoFundMe drive? Who said I was the best mentor he'd ever had? Who said I was like a father figure, since his own father left his East St. Louis family before he was born. That Ke'Von?

"…all right, Ke'Von, sounding good, but a little too much like Monroe, and you're like a younger, hipper Monroe, but still with a Black edge…Do the intro again."

"Good evening, L.A. I'm Ke'Von Carrington. This is *Live at Five*. Our top story comes from the city of South Pasadena, where…"

I'm Justin Monroe. I keep everyone afloat. I work hard.

I've earned my spot. I've kept *More at Four with Justin Monroe* and *Live at Five* number one in L.A. for almost sixteen years. I finished my doctorate in journalism, which I barely let my news colleagues know, because I know what they'd think. Black. Uppity. Smart. Thinks he knows more than us. Where's one of Elijah's breathing exercises when I need them?

I step into the studio. "What is this? Did I miss the memo?"

❖

Two hours later, I'm sitting in my SUV in the station parking lot and about to make my way back home to Ladera Heights. I barely remember bits of conversation like "new direction," "fresh start," "appeal to our more conservative viewers," "compete with digital news," and other statements that come with the territory of new corporate owners, new station management, and new ways that people get their news. And the cherry on top—an offer for me to anchor weekends at six and eleven or weekdays at noon—is the equivalent of putting the old horse out to pasture in the news business.

So much for sixteen years at number one.

I park in my driveway. See Trevor's car in his driveway next door. Young ones gone. Elijah gone. Brenda up in Sacramento. Only one place to go and vent. Trevor's.

After I reply to my young ones' text messages that I miss them, that I'm glad they've arrived safely at their grandparents in Brooklyn, have they heard from their mother, and to let me know if they need anything Zelled to them, I'm standing outside Trevor's front door. I give a courtesy knock, even though I could use the spare key he keeps in the lockbox on the side of the house.

"Hey," Trevor says when he opens the door. "I wasn't expecting you."

"I need to talk to someone." I walk into the front hall. "You won't believe the day I've had."

"Um, you won't believe the day I'm having," Trevor says, holding an unopened bottle of Corner 103 Pinot Noir. I smell what reminds me of Sunday dinner, but on a Saturday, in the air. I know Trevor doesn't cook. Then I put it together. A date.

"Is someone here?"

"Sonoma's here," he whispers. "We're kinda getting back together."

"Oh. Well…get back to your man. I guess."

"What were you going to tell me?" Trevor says. "But make it quick, if you catch my drift, buddy. You know I love you, but Sonoma's about to plate dinner. He cooked."

Buddy. And here we go again with the *love* word. Ugh.

"It's okay, Trevor. Enjoy your date. We can talk another time."

"I'm sorry, Justin. Forgive me this one time."

"Forgive you for what, babe?" I hear Sonoma's voice coming near the front hallway where Trevor and I are trying to have a discreet bestie conversation. "Something wrong?"

Finally, Sonoma emerges from Trevor's kitchen, shirtless with gray joggers on. He wraps his arms around Trevor from behind and presses into Trevor, placing a few small pecks on Trevor's neck.

Sonoma isn't just some "regular" guy, as Trevor had shared with me in one of our previous wine downs. I recognize Sonoma guy's face as a supporting actor from one of those Tyler Perry soaps my sister Brenda and my mom and aunties watch. I give a quick up-and-down look and think he's lighter, shorter, and thinner than I imagined him to be from the few times I've seen him on screen. All of us who work on television look different in real life. He's definitely a good ten to fifteen years younger than Trevor.

"Sonoma," Trevor says. "This is my longest and best friend Justin. Justin, Sonoma."

So, I guess his name isn't just from the wine country where they've gone on long weekends. Well, this is funny and awkward.

"Sup, bestie," Sonoma says and smiles. Puts a hand out. "Heard lots about you. Seen you on TV, too. You're smart."

"Same." We shake hands. I want to say *but you're not smart, just a pretty face,* but I won't be jealous or mean. Jealous, maybe. "Sorry to interrupt your hangout."

"It's good," Trevor and Sonoma say at the same time. And laugh. Then they plant a small kiss on each other's lips.

"It's all right," I say. Awkward. My best friend and crush looks happy, even though last time I remember, Trevor was through with Sonoma. Confusion aside, I don't want to crash this party. "I'ma head home. I stay next door, Sonoma. I can talk with you later, Trevor."

"You ain't gotta rush. I made enough for three or four, if you want to stay, and we've got plenty of wine. But I understand if you don't."

"Yeah, we can talk later, Justin," Trevor says, gives me a little eye that best friends give when they want you to leave, and backs up tighter into Sonoma's arms. "If you know what I mean, best friend."

"Enjoy." I back up onto the front porch. "See you when I see you."

The front door closes with a gentle slam. Through the stained glass window of the door, I see the silhouettes of Trevor and Sonoma face, embrace, and kiss each other. I guess I'll write this one off as a loss.

I cross Trevor's front yard to mine. I get in my SUV and dial Elijah. I don't know where I'm planning on driving on a

Saturday evening, but I'm definitely not staying home while my bestie and crush entertains Sonoma tonight.

"Wait, wasn't I supposed to call you tomorrow, Uncle J?"

"Yeah, but things have changed."

"What does that mean?"

"Fuck it," I say and start up the truck. "I might join you for one or two days in Miami. That's a might. I'll do my own travel and accommodations if I do."

"But I thought you were going to be *busy* relaxing or *busy* working on some story."

"Nephew," I go. "Busy ain't the half of it."

CHAPTER FOUR

Elijah: This Isn't The Right Time

Zaire, I'm not ready to move in with you. Please stop sending me Zillow apartments. Love, it's just not the right time.
I copy this prewritten message from the secured notes app I have in my phone and place it in a text message to the love of my life, Zaire. Yes, this would make for a better conversation in person, but I don't have time right now. I'm preparing for one of the biggest auditions I've ever had. I'm an hour and a half northwest of Los Angeles, in the small city of Ojai, California, at my Uncle Justin's getaway property. He has allowed me to stay here for a few days to center myself and properly prepare for this opportunity. I love it here. I'm secluded from the outside world. Everything I currently need to help me focus I have right here with me: indoor gym, swimming pool, stocked refrigerator, script, silence, and spotty Wi-Fi.

My regular phone number has been turned off for the week, and I'm only operating via email or my free Google number. Only the essential people have access to my Google number: the parentals, mommy and daddy Golden, my love Zaire, Uncle J, my best friends Ezra and Lenay, and my agent Lyrique. Outside of the morning text from the parentals, they all know to contact me only when absolutely necessary. So, when the fourth text message pops up on my laptop, all coming from Zaire, and interrupts me from practicing this tedious scene, I realize I need him to know I do not want to look at another one bedroom apartment on *Zillow*. Especially not now, when I was finally tapping into the energy I wanted to express in the scene.

I am ready to press send on that text. But I do not.

I try not to operate from a space of frustration, and that's exactly where I'm sending this message from. Frustration. I stop recording myself on the laptop. I get up from the living room office desk, walk to the ceiling-to-floor window wall, and stare at the backyard. I'd love to be able to afford a home like this. I wouldn't necessarily want to live here in Ojai; suburban life isn't specifically for me at this moment, but being here right now feels good. Although I'm primarily here to really study this scene, I'm also here to get away from my rapid routine in normal life.

The life I have is mostly my creation, the manifestation of what I want, so this isn't a complaint. I'm grateful to be living the life I've assisted in creating. However, it can be a bit much at times.

I'm an actor. Theater and acting are my passions. My first paid gig was at the age of seven. I did an Oscar Mayer commercial, but it wasn't until middle school theatre that I really fell in love with acting. Lyrique sends me on auditions, and I have acting classes twice a week. Three days a week, I teach a morning spinning class that also helps keep me fit, and on top of that, some of Jus's and Junior's classmates' parents pay me to tutor math and prep them for standardized texts. Between tutoring, spin class, and the few small gigs I get with acting, mostly commercials and being an extra in some tiny productions, I manage fine financially, despite Uncle Justin having his checkbook open to me anytime I want.

I've had this routine for about three years now, and I've

met wonderful people during this time. My schedule didn't seem to get in the way of anything until recently because I haven't adapted it to fit my love life. I haven't changed up my routine since Zaire and I have flowed into this entanglement.

Okay, it's not an entanglement. It's a relationship. I'm just frustrated that I haven't had the conversation to move in or to not move in with each other. Our relationship is tender, monogamous, romantic, sweet, and fun.

When he and I first started talking—dating, I was having a great summer of a rainbow of intimacies, all different names and places. Then as time went on, I found myself sharing more time and energy with him and less with all the others. And there were a few others: Gia the guitarist, Tori the teacher, Luke the lawyer, and Brex the barbeque guy. But it was Zaire the zaddy who got me most.

Between auditions, I'd send Zaire a selfie with four words to describe how I felt the audition went. I'd send a grinning selfie with *That just wasn't it*, a side-eye selfie with *Yup, they could never!*, or a whatever face with a *Love to see it*. Rarely did my expressions and captions make sense with each other. That wasn't the point. He was so encouraging. This was the first time I let someone from outside my intimate circle into my craft world, my passion world. I loved that he had no interest or connection in entertainment. Yet he had time and space for me when I needed or wanted that. Two years later, he still makes time and space for me.

I open my phone to look at the four one-bedroom apartments he sent me. They are all nice. Affordable even. Mostly affordable if I accept his offer for us to equitably share the cost of living together. Things wouldn't be fifty-fifty, but rather based on how much we make. And he works in social media and tech, so technically, he currently makes more than me. Moving in with each other makes sense financially. We like and love each other. He has a toothbrush at my apartment. I have thongs at his. For some, this next stage of living together would be an easy transition, but, for me, it's fucking scary.

I fear us becoming strangers if we move in with each other. I've seen and studied people become strangers to someone they've known, loved, for years, over and over again, like my Uncle Justin and Aunt Jeanine. It is possible and easy to be a stranger to someone you know deeply. Sometimes in many parts of one day I am a stranger with myself. I do something that I would have sworn I'd never do, or I think of things that I've never thought about before, and in those moments, I am a stranger to myself.

I find myself learning and enjoying that stranger most times, but every once in a while, that stranger leaves me knowing I may not ever know someone else the way I think I need, to give myself completely. Moving in with a partner feels this way to me. Giving myself, receiving someone, being tethered. Additionally, with this tethered cohabitation, there's this c-word I struggle with—compromise. I have very little space to compromise in my life outside of work. I think underneath all of this is what Ezra calls my only child syndrome having a tantrum.

I get to the final apartment, which is actually a loft in downtown L.A. with tall windows and a high ceiling. It's much bigger than both of our apartments combined, enough space to actually have two bedrooms. It's hearted/marked as favorite in his list of apartments. It feels like he's been noticing all the things I like about homes and apartments. This warms my heart. I can't forget I am scared of living together, but I appreciate the tenderness of this romantic experience.

Thus, before texting Zaire my original text, I think with my better sense. I text Ezra. They'll let me know if I'm sabotaging myself or not. I don't want to be the last to know if I am.

❖

I've recorded the monologue a dozen times, each time a little different than the other. An eyebrow raise this time. An inflection here. An inflection there. Try a slight head nod. More blinks. Less blink. No blinks. Slow the words. Speed up the last line. I don't know which one to go with. All twelve are okay, but they each give a different vibe.

I call it enough rehearsing for the day. I close my laptop just enough for the screen to darken. Then I walk to the giant-ass kitchen to scavenge food in the refrigerator. Uncle J had one of his assistants restock the fridge with a few of my favorite things: fresh produce, kombucha, fresh seafood. I'm so grateful. My family says I eat like a bird. Meh. I'm just not a foodie. I'm pretty simple. I pull out the fish, asparagus, butter, lemon, one sweet potato, and a garlic clove. Once seasoned, the fish, the sweet potato, and the asparagus will go into the oven at different times. First the potato, which takes the longest, then the fish and asparagus. This is a quick and delicious meal.

As I wait for the fish to cook, I have *Hey Google* play one of my favorite podcasts—*Modern Love*. I love this podcast. Writers submit stories centering on romantic and platonic love, and actors read the stories. The one that's playing is a story about a woman's visit to a psychic and her questioning the arrival of death. It's read by Queen Mother Angela Bassett. Her conviction and command for attention is unmatched. One day, I'd like to be an actor who reads one of the stories. Maybe read my own story, even. The gall.

When the food is cooked and plated, I open the wine cabinet or, as Uncle Justin calls it, his *cellaret*, and pour a glass of Cabernet, just one pour. I take a sip and it's warm and smooth as velvet going down my throat. Angela is still melodically speaking as a doorbell sounds. For a moment, I think it's someone at the door, but I dismiss the idea because I'm more sure it's the story, and I just zoomed out for a second. Then Queen Mother Angela finishes, and the podcast goes on a quick break. The doorbell sounds again. This time, I'm certain someone's here. I almost leave whoever it is at the door because I'm not expecting a guest. But then I realize the white, affluent, nosy neighbors aren't used to activity in the house, so it could be them. Or the cops checking in. So I reluctantly head to the door, taking off my du-rag, just in case it is indeed the cops.

I open the door.

"Surprise, love!" Zaire says as he hands me my favorite flower—sunflowers.

I'm pleasantly relieved it wasn't a nosy-ass neighbor or a cop, but I do have a shook look on my face.

Zaire enters and kisses me on the cheek.

"I know you're not a fan of surprises like this," Zaire says. "I just couldn't get past the fact that I didn't get a chance to see you before you drove up here because I couldn't step out of my damn meeting."

Zaire leads the way down the long hallway to the kitchen. He knows this place. He's been invited...before.

He's right. I don't like surprises. Him popping up at Kitchen 24 to walk me home was cute. It was him knowing I was drunk as a skunk and wouldn't mind him walking me home. Him popping up here, unannounced, not so cute. In general, there are some people who love surprises. Take Ezra, for example. They *love* surprises—gifts, parties, pop-ups. Zaire too. Me, I like to know. I think it's less about actual surprises and more about preparation and structure.

Being with Zaire, I've really learned to be open to adventures. But he usually at least gives me a heads-up. Like he'll say, Saturday, at set time, be ready to go. And I can work with that because it allows me to mentally prepare for the unknown to happen at a specific time.

"Zaire..." I finally say when we make it to the kitchen.

"I know. I know, love. I didn't tell you I was coming. I won't stay long. I know this weekend is for you to Zen out and prepare."

"Right."

I stare at him looking at me. He looks sexy, per usual. He's wearing a nicely fitted purple polo shirt and light blue slim pants. He knows I'm trying to look more bothered than I actually am.

"Love me through it," he says in a scratchy high tone, which is a saying he says when he wants me to laugh and accept whatever he has done.

I laugh. How could I not laugh? I walk over to him from the other side of the kitchen and kiss him on the lips.

"I just made some food for dinner," I say. "Made enough for leftovers, but I suppose you can have the other portion."

I make him a plate. We eat at the dining table. We sit next to each other and play footsies.

❖

After we eat, we chill in the living room for a few moments, with the Apple TV showing an animal documentary show. We like Discovery Channel things. Then he starts kissing me. I get up from the sofa, grab the silk sofa throw, and place it on the ground, because we are about to get down.

I take off my shorts. I only wear them when I'm in the

house, because they show my cheeks at times. I'm not wearing underwear. He strips down to his briefs and socks. We start to have sex.

He whispers slow and deep, "You like that don't you?"

He kisses my neck from the back.

"You love it, don't you?" he says, going deeper.

And I do.

I moan and bite my lip.

"Yes," I gasp. "Yes, I love it."

The after-sex feeling is rejuvenating. I could easily lie here and cuddle in all of our juices. It is so easy to be still with Zaire. We tend to do that when we have nothing in particular to do after we have sex. Both of us aren't quick to get towels or freshen up. I sometimes like to allow whatever liquids I have on or in me to just be there. Sometimes I smear the remains on my stomach or chest. Sometimes I lick it off my fingers or off him. Sometimes the cuddling and the smearing leads to more sex. I start to rub his wet chest, then I stop because the cuddling will *not* lead to more sex. I'm not here to enjoy the ambience. I have work to do. I unwrap his arm from around me and head to the bathroom to take a quick shower. This will show him I'm still in my work mode, and he's on a timer. He said he wasn't staying long. He's been here a few hours, and he has about an hour-and-a-half drive home.

"You have two texts from Ezra on your laptop," I hear Zaire yell from the same spot we just made spontaneous love in the living room.

I love the huge walk-in shower with the rainfall showerhead here. The perks of television success. Before the water heats up and I submerge myself underneath the rainfall, I ask him to read the texts aloud. The water heats within seconds and the steam starts to rise. I walk into the water.

"I can't hear you," I shout after a few seconds go by without Zaire saying a word.

"Zaire, what is the text?" I say.

"It said," Zaire says as he enters the bathroom, "talk to him. In person, gurl! And just so you know, I haven't forgotten. When you get back, we can talk about Jordan."

CHAPTER FIVE

Justin: Across State Lines

"I'm about to go in for the parent Senior Prep Day," I say as I'm pulling past security into the gates of the Hills Academy, where my young ones are soon beginning their fourth year of high school. Jus and Junior are on speaker with me now. "Is there anything I need to know so I'm not surprised?"

I'm imagining the eye rolls from both of my young ones. But I don't care. I miss them. Terribly. And it's just day three of their East Coast vacation with the grandparents. Apparently, they're in D.C. visiting Howard University today. I really just wanted to hear their voices.

"Dad, chill," Junior says. "We gucci. We good."

"Is that so, young man?" I say, consciously deciding to forgo telling him the "are" was missing. We *are* good.

"Yes sir," Junior says. "Maybe you can talk to them about making the school a little more Black, though. It's boring."

"That part, Dad," Jus says. "And it doesn't make sense since we have a new principal at the Hills who's Black."

"That's weird," I say. "How come no one told me that before?"

"That's what you pay cousin Elijah for, to keep you updated on our school matters," Junior says. "But whatever."

That hurts. I don't neglect them. The twins know how

busy I am and that Elijah is a willing assistant to them and to me when we need it.

"If anything, Dad, you should be prepared for the weirdness of our teachers," Jus says. "You usually send cousin Elijah to the school, and I don't know if they know you're *the* Justin Monroe. They're going to freak out."

Jus and Junior can be a little naive about having a public figure for a father, but their teachers have to know who I am. That's what Google is for. I also know I'm not the only well-known parent of a Hills Academy student. This place shields my young ones from the army of fake news crazies out there who will look for any excuse to harm me for something I've reported. Not just anyone can afford the amount of tuition, room, and board for high school, and a lot of us are paying for the safety, privacy, and anonymity so that our young ones can be somewhat normal around other teens who have high-profile and monied parents.

Truth be told, I also know there are no surprises coming when I go inside. Jus and Junior are angels at home and in school. They're both close to straight-A students. The therapists, counselors, and psychiatrists all expected otherwise once their mother left just before the twins started high school. My family—mainly my older sister Brenda—thought the kids and I would fall apart after Jeanine found her bliss with the woman of her dreams. Three years come and go so fast. But we good, as Junior likes to say.

"It's just going to be an in and out quick visit with a few teachers anyway," I say. "I've decided to meet up with your cousin Elijah in Miami for a few days. Leaving tonight."

"That's awesome, Dad," Jus says. She's always so positive. "You need a break. I'm happy for you. Who's going to watch after all those damn plants in Elijah's apartment?"

"Did I hear you swear in my presence, young lady?"

Celeste, their grandmother, intervenes in the background. I hope Celeste doesn't think I'm a bad parent.

"Apologize to your grandma, Jus," I say.

"Sorry, Grandma," Jus quickly replies.

I allow the kids to use the language they need to express themselves when they're with me. I guess they forgot the rest of the world expects formalities from young ones. Besides, they get the damn cursing from me.

"Thanks, Jus," I say. "If you all were here, I'd let you house-sit for Elijah—and water all those damn plants."

We laugh over our little rebellious moment against Grandma Celeste.

"But we're on the East Coast, Dad, duh." Another zinger from Junior, who's determined to show me I'm his worst enemy anytime he can. I don't take the bait.

"If you all end up in Florida A&M land with your grandparents while I'm in Miami, let me know," I say. I'm not trying to be a needy parent, but I am. Even when they resist me with all their teenage angst and drama. "Maybe I'll catch a quick flight up to Tallahassee."

"No way in hell we're going to college in Florida, RIP Trayvon," Jus says. "Despite the latest report somewhere putting FAMU on the top of the HBCU list. Eff that."

"We got this, Dad," Junior says. "Besides, you need to take lessons from Uncle Trevor and get *some* in Miami. Elijah got cute friends, too. JK, dad." Junior lets out a laugh.

"What did you just say?" I ask.

"You need to get some, Dad," Junior says. "Release. Smash. Bang."

"Where are your grandparents right now?"

"They're here in the room next door to us being nosy with that door open between our rooms like we can't be trusted," Junior goes. "Anything else?"

"You're only sixteen. You're talking like you know grown folks' business."

"It was a joke."

"You can't joke like that," I say. "Celeste and Henry are going to think I'm not raising you right."

And the last thing I want is not having Jus and Junior in my life on a daily basis because Jeanine's parents lose trust in me.

Probably the one thing I've done wrong, if you can call it that, in the three years since Jeanine left is to let the village help raise my twins. Time and the TV station, you know? But I'm not neglectful. Brenda, my sister, flies down from Sacramento to help out a few times a year when she and I aren't arguing over her son, Elijah, who prefers to live nearer me than her. Elijah runs them around on their errands and dates when he's not on one of his auditions or jobs or mental wellness retreats. Celeste and Henry take them on some holidays. I've hired and had a few personal assistants, housekeepers, tutors, and coaches over the past few years to help me help them while I'm busy keeping everyone afloat.

Speaking of keeping everyone afloat, when do I tell the family that I'm being demoted at the station? That in just a few weeks—well, kinda now—I'm no longer the lead anchor of the four and five o'clock newscasts. Embarrassing and maddening. I think I'll wait until the twins are back in L.A. in a couple weeks and tell them first, then the rest of the Monroes, then Celeste and Henry before the story makes its way to social media.

"Love you, Dad," Jus says, snapping me out of my personal reflection. "We're off now to tour Kamala's alma mater and to have dinner later with some faculty Grandma and Granddad know. They're summoning us now."

"All right, enjoy," I go. "And—"

Silence. Disconnected. Teenagers.
And I'm parking.

❖

It's a warm summer morning, definitely warmer here in Burbank than it is closer to the water in Ladera Heights as I'm wandering outside the administration building of the Hills Academy. Been out here for a good five or seven minutes trying to find the main door to the building. Being Black, male, and solo, not necessarily the smartest thing to do outside an exclusive school for young people of the rich and well-known. I know I'm not a frequent visitor, but I also thought I'd been here enough to recognize the front door.

"Can I help you, young man?" I hear a male voice call out to me from behind. Certainly, he's being sarcastic and mistaken. I'm nowhere near being a young man. I turn around. He is definitely mistaken. "I mean, sir. I mean, hellooooo."

Means he recognizes me. Brown eyes widening and showing me all thirty-two of his pearly whites, which contrast beautifully with his glowing skin, the shade of dark brown.

"Hi, I'm Justin Monroe," I say, sounding more TV anchorman than concerned parent. I extend a hand, but then transition into an elbow bump. I'm a bit of a germaphobe at times. My eyes wander to the fitted yellow polo shirt he's wearing, with the forest green Hills Academy logo embossed over his left pec. Someone works out, I think, but I bring myself back to the matter at hand. Parent-teacher conferences. "My young ones go here."

"I'm the new headmaster slash principal here, Dr. Jabari Braxton," he says. "But you can call me Jabari or Dr. Braxton. Whatever you're comfortable with. Wow, you sound exactly like you do on..."

Sometimes I forget people know who I am because I work on TV, and that makes people nervous at times to meet "somebody famous." But I just try and put them at ease with a smile. Like I do now.

"Good to meet, Dr. Jabari Braxton," I say. And in my head, I'm thinking good name for television news. Good face and body for—let me stop. Three plus years without some is a long time. Maybe I do need to smash, as Junior says. "Just call me Justin. Or whatever you're comfortable with."

"Justice and Justin Monroe, right? Your young scholars?"

"Right. And you know because…"

"Elijah, your nephew, right? He talks about you every time he's here at the Hills, as we call it unofficially. We've become close. Friends, I guess you could say."

"Oh, that Elijah. Always making friends."

"I'm trying not to fangirl, I mean fanboy," Jabari says, grin still plastered across his face. Even with his rich dark complexion, I notice the red undertones on his face, letting me know he is in fact blushing. "But Elijah has kind of turned me into a fan for all you do."

"Nice. Elijah *is* my favorite and only nephew."

"He's always telling me about your generosity," Jabari says. He's smiling and I'm smiling inside a little at his smiling and eye contact with me. Being fangirled or fanboyed never gets old. And when it's from someone as nice looking as this Jabari, I mean, Dr. Braxton, it's even better. "And how you're helping support his acting career. Your outings and rituals when you find time to relax from the busy-ness of your life. And I hear it's pretty busy. Not that I'm in your business or anything."

I want to say *but you are trying to be*. Instead, I go, "I'm amazed about all this talking Elijah does, when he should be focusing on my young ones and their progress in school.

Which, by the way, is why you caught me out here wandering looking for an open door. Where's everyone at for the Parent-Teacher conference or Senior Prep Day for parents?"

"Ha," Jabari says. Lets out a little chuckle. "Senior Prep Day was yesterday."

"Shit, yesterday?" I ask in a way that's accusing myself of bad parenting for forgetting. I pull out my phone and check the schedule. It's definitely marked for today. Obviously a mistake. "How did I miss that?"

"It happens a lot," Jabari goes. "Especially with the parents at the Hills."

"I'm not trying to be like the parents of the Hills," I say. I'm embarrassed. "Shit, I *am* one of those parents."

"No worries. I'm here today closing up campus so the staff and I can enjoy these last weeks off for summer break. However, we could set up a call or a Zoom or a FaceTime if you want. I wouldn't mind filling you in."

"But my young ones are off for two more weeks," I say. "Or did I get that wrong, too? I just want to make sure I'm set with everything I have to do for their senior year."

"The staff is off for one more week, then next week is for teacher preparation for fall," Jabari says. "We'll set something up."

"Got it. Damn, I feel stupid. Sorry for interrupting your school closing tasks. I coulda saved this time to pack and get to the airport. Traffic's about to be a mess."

"Miami? Elijah's trip? You're going?"

"Yeah, how'd you know?" But then I don't have to bother asking why. The loosest lips of the West Coast, other than my sister Brenda. "My nephew confided that in you, too. Ha."

"Not so much, but he invited me. I'm on an overnight flight."

"Oh, did he?" I'm going to have to talk to Elijah about

being so damn friendly with everyone, especially on a vacation I wasn't even planning to go on. "Small world."

"Not that we want to talk shop or young ones in Miami," Jabari goes. "But maybe we can talk shop or young ones in Miami. For a little bit."

"That's funny. But then again, multitasking, doing too much, making efficient use of time, that's me."

"Then we're on." He smiles.

"We're on." I smile back.

MIAMI

83° | Humidity 75%

CHAPTER SIX

Justin: Bienvenido a Miami

I'll tell you one thing: Miami is too damn hot and humid and moist, reasons number one, two, and three why I don't vacation here.

Tropical isn't my thing. Neither is the so-called dry heat, which is ironic, considering that I grew up in Sacramento and live in L.A. now, where dry heat is getting hotter by the day thanks to climate change and global warming.

Even when Jeanine and I got married almost twenty years ago, shortly after our respective doctoral programs ended, we didn't do the typical "go to an island, book an all-inclusive resort, hang out and drink with other young newlywed couples by the pool by day and dance silly line dances" kind of honeymoon because of our combined disdain for heat.

Instead, we found a small Black-owned bed and breakfast on the coast of Maine, where we were able to nerd out and relax with our respective research, writing, and job searches—Jeanine in academia and mine in television news. Not much honeymooning, if you know what I mean. That was a clue to something we'd eventually admit to ourselves and learn to live with. We were both queer, questioning, and on a quest to find our true selves in our marriage arrangement.

Last time I was near Miami was in 2018 when the station flew me over this way to cover voter suppression efforts in the South and to look for connections to anything remotely similar in L.A. That was back when my station was owned by a real news organization. First, I covered Georgia and the Stacey Abrams gubernatorial campaign. Then I came down to Miami to report on the shenanigans that kept Andrew Gillum out of the governor's office in Florida. Allegedly. Always have to say *allegedly* to avoid getting sued, even though we all knew and know it to be true.

After the assignment was over and I filed my stories, I stayed one extra day and night. I drove south, so I could experience Miami's gay nightlife as a newly free and figuring-out-my-life man. Didn't know anyone or anywhere to go, so when I typed in *gay* and *Miami* and *night life* into a search engine, all that came up for me to try were a few clubs with mostly shirtless white or white-presenting men, fast-paced beats without words or singing, and obvious and hidden drug use on and off the dance floor. Plus, no one talked to me. It turned me off. Not that I'm particularly judgmental. I've seen it all working in TV news, and nothing surprises me. At the time, and even now, what I experienced in Miami a few years back just wasn't what or how I wanted to spend my adult years.

So, Miami today. It's still not high on my list, but it's my role as a loving uncle to show up and be supportive and spend a few days with Elijah, his partner Zaire, and his cast of friends and acquaintances on their *Miami Gone Wild* trip. Trust, Justin Monroe will not be going wild. I want to relax. It's not often I get free time—no work, no young ones, no research, no obligations, no news anchor voice, cadence, and diction to perform.

As the car pulls up to the house Elijah rented, I ring him on his cell.

"I'm here, nephew."

"Awesome, Uncle J," Elijah shouts. "On my way out to meet you!"

Sometimes, I swear Elijah's more like nine years old than twenty-nine or whatever he is. But his youthful energy and kind spirit are what have endeared him to me over the years. I decide to wait with the driver in the air-conditioned car until Elijah makes his way outside, as I'm not in the mood for melting in the Miami heat.

The house looks a little underwhelming for my taste and budget. I mean, for a house in a gated community adjacent to a private beach, the front yard greenery looks a little overgrown and shabby, the stucco could use a paint touch-up, and the overall curb appeal is blah compared to some of the other homes and modern architecture and new construction we passed along the way in this subdivision. I know Elijah isn't exactly rolling in the dough, so I will keep my judgment to myself, and pray that he hasn't been taken by an unscrupulous Airbnb owner.

The front door opens and Elijah, shirtless, but with a red cup in hand, sprints outside to the car in peach-colored swim shorts, flip-flops, and sunglasses. He could use a support garment under those swim shorts, because he's flopping everywhere. He looks like he's been in the sun all day, too, which is the reason people come to Miami, I guess. I tap the app to pay the driver and get out to greet my nephew.

"Bienvenidos a Miami," Elijah goes in broken but passable Spanish. It's something we do, being born and raised in California, no matter who you are—speak some kind of Spanish. "I'm so glad you're here, Uncle J."

"Hey, nephew." I smile. We hug. Not too long. It's hot. I'm hot standing here. He's glistening. I'm not sure if it's sweat or some kind of tanning oil, but I don't want it on me. "Looks like you're enjoying yourself already."

"I am," he says and holds up his cup. "We need to get you a drink. 'Cause we been drinking since this morning and you need to catch up. The white Henny is kinda litty."

"Love it, Elijah."

"How was the flight? When'd you get in? Let me help you with your bags."

The car drives off. Elijah looks confused.

"No bags. I got my own hotel. No drama or anything."

"Buzz kill."

"Just want you and your friends to feel like you can be yourselves on your *Miami Gone Wild* trip without the Uncle J energy killing the vibe. And you know Brenda will be calling me wanting a play-by-play about everything going on here. No Vegas rule for her."

The truth is, I just booked my hotel room from the plane. Once the thought settled in my mind that Dr. Braxton, my twins' principal, was staying in the Airbnb with Elijah and company, I thought about a potential conflict of interest. The last thing I want is drama for myself, my young ones, or for the school's lead administrator.

"Oh, whatever," Elijah puts his free hand up into an L. "You're my favorite uncle. My crew knows you're like one of my best friends. But whatever. That's all right. Come on in."

"Thanks for understanding," I say, as we walk up the front sidewalk and through the front door. "Plus, I never relax and just do nothing. You and Trevor both been on me about trying something different with my life. So, I'm here. That's different."

Elijah and I started out the year with a resolution to be

each other's accountability partners—me for consistency with his acting and settling down after years of start-and-stop relationships, him for consistency with my leisure, as if I can really enjoy leisure with sixteen-year-old twins, and for me starting to date again.

"Oh wow, this is nice," I say, looking around the house.

"What's that supposed to mean, Uncle J? Are you surprised?"

"I mean, the front of the house is a little..."

What the house lacks on the outside, it definitely makes up inside with HGTV-like design vibes. I see an open floor plan, clean lines, and a straight shot view of the patio and pool area in the back, where his crew, Ezra, Lenay, and a few others I don't recognize are lounging.

"Where's Zaire? I mean, this is your post-audition-of-a-lifetime celebration, right?"

"That's the appeal. No Zaire on this trip. And another gig I didn't get."

"Is there a story about Zaire? Sounds like you're spending more time apart than you are together. Is he still a part of your life?"

"Are you on assignment for *More at Four* or *Live at Five*? It's okay for us to have separate but equal lives. Chill." Elijah rolls his eyes. He's lucky he's my nephew and not some smart-mouthed stranger. Otherwise... He shifts back to vacation mode quickly. "Anyway, let's go out back and link up with everyone."

"Or you can stay inside and cool off for a minute," says the soothing, deep voice that greeted me at my young ones' school the other day. "With me."

It's Jabari. Good old principal and new friend of my nephew who magically was invited on this trip. He hands me a glass.

"I made you a drink," Jabari says, smiling and staring. "Hope you don't mind me assuming you like it dark."

Sounds like something Trevor would say. Another flirt who specializes in double entendre. Original.

"Ooop," Elijah says and starts off toward the back of the house. "I'm going to refresh while you two…relax. You know where to find us. And no mention of Zaire on this trip. Thank you."

Last time I saw Jabari, he was looking semi-professional in the yellow fitted polo that's part of the Hills Academy uniform look. Today, Jabari is practically naked in front of me, wearing just yellow Speedo swim trunks—and there's no deceiving what he's carrying, if you know what I mean.

And everything I wondered about Jabari underneath the yellow polo is just as I imagined him without it: broad chest and shoulders, flat abs with a hint of a six-pack, tapered waist, and a vee that leads down to the yellow trunks. He knows what colors look good on his dark skin. And he looks more like he should be dancing on a pole than leading a school as a principal. That's for sure.

Jabari holds up his drink and clinks it to mine.

"Cheers to Miami," he says. "I'm glad you made it. You do like it dark, I hope?"

"Cheers," I say. "We're supposed to talk shop—my young ones. Remember?"

"Come on, Justin. You and I both know your young ones are doing just fine at the Hills. Making excellent grades. Highly involved. Pretty popular. Blah, blah, blah."

"Thanks for your highly detailed report on my young ones. I feel like I got my forty grand's worth from you right now."

"Ha. You're funny."

"I try. But in all seriousness, Jabari, my young ones don't

really like it at the Hills anymore. They feel like you don't do enough to make campus feel welcoming for Black students. I pay too much money for my young ones not to be happy."

"Well, tell me how you really feel," Jabari says. "I mean, how your kids really feel."

"Just saying. Not trying to put a damper on this…"

"This?"

"Vacation," I say and smile. "Not 'this' as in 'us.'"

"There's an 'us'?" Jabari flashes that smile again that makes me wanna…

"No 'us.'"

"Aww, I'm hurt," he says. "Anyway, I don't know about you, Justin, but I didn't come to Miami to talk about students. And especially knowing yours aren't too happy about me or the school."

"You promised me a talk shop moment when we were back in Burbank. Especially since I missed Senior Prep Day for parents."

"I'm on break. And to be honest, I'd rather talk about you."

"Me?"

"You." He motions to a nearby sectional, where he places a hand towel from an adjacent basket down first before sitting and covering himself up with another towel. "You. Continue."

"Wow, good drink," I say after finally taking a sip of the cocktail Jabari handed me when I arrived at the house. "This is strong."

"Thanks. I'm good at things other than giving highly detailed parent-teacher conference reports."

"If you say so, Jabari."

"I do. Now back to you, Justin."

"So much for subtlety." I'm flattered Jabari is such a heavy flirt, but I don't think Jus and Junior would be happy with me entertaining their principal. "I guess that's what app life and the app generation are all about, huh? You just risk it all."

"Are you judging?"

"I'm sorry if that's what it seems like," I say. "We barely know each other, but I just think you're coming across a little…I don't want to say strong or desperate. So, I'll just say youngish. Not trying to hurt your feelings, Mr. Braxton."

"Doctor, since we're being formal."

"Well, I've got a doctorate, too," I say. "Since we're throwing out formalities."

"I guess I should be polite to my elders."

Wait. How did we go from zero to a hundred in a matter of seconds? "You're the one showing your age and immaturity, Dr. Braxton."

"Well, if you really want to know, Dr. Monroe, I'm turning thirty-eight on this trip," he says. The age shocks me. I took him for maybe thirty, thirty-one, somewhere around Elijah's age, but then again, I guess I shouldn't assume anything these days. "And there's guys older than us on the apps, by the way."

Not that I'd know. I mean, how would that look, someone of my career status and notoriety on a dating or hookup app. It's bad enough all the non-disclosure documents and background checks I have to ask new staff or assistants, a potential friend who's not in the news business, or a possible date to do. No one wants to go through all that just for a chance to be in my world. I do, however, trust my nephew's friends on this trip. I also trust the people I grew up with in Sacramento, my family, and the people who knew me when I was just Justin, and not *the* Justin Monroe. And, of course, I have to assume Jabari's passed a criminal record screening since he's the headmaster at my young ones' high school.

But I digress.

"Well, happy birthday season, Jabari. Thirty-eight looks

good on you. And I apologize. That escalated quickly. Not my style."

"Thanks," he says. "Apology accepted."

We raise our glasses. We smile. We toast.

I'm close to thinking I like this Dr. Jabari Braxton. Not in the same, long-term and longing way that I like Trevor back in L.A., but in a "he's fascinating, he's showing interest, he's educated, he's got a fire personality" kinda way. And we've done nothing but have two random conversations.

"But if I do the math correctly, given your accomplishments and the ages of the other parents of the teens at the Hills, you're probably mid-forties, maybe a bit more?"

"Jabari, I work in television in L.A. You know we don't talk age. But you're in the range-ish, if you want to know."

And you're age appropriate, as Elijah would tell me about this dating possibility, but I wouldn't dare say that out loud now to Jabari or anyone.

"Higher or lower?" he says, smiling. "I mean, I could have googled you or just looked in the campus files, but I didn't want to go on record violating some FERPA shit, though your young ones are minors and FERPA doesn't count in high school."

"Oh yeah," I say, and I'm out of the clouds and back to reality. "You are my young ones' principal. Aren't there rules about that?"

"About what?"

Not about to show my cards that I might have a feeling or a tingle. "Never mind, Jabari."

"Yeah, you're right," Jabari says. "That's enough shop talk. You're one of my parents, anyway. And your young ones apparently don't like the job I'm doing. But answer me this, Justin."

"What?"

"Higher or lower?"

"That's all you're getting from me for now," I say. We clink glasses. "Maybe later."

"Promise?"

"Elijah, Lenay, Ezra, and them are going to wonder why we disappeared and are hanging out in the house."

"I'm cool. They cool. You cool?"

"I'm definitely cool," I say. "Just relaxing and enjoying this drink. And this air conditioning. I hate hot."

"So, then you hate me?" He laughs and sticks out his tongue. "That's a joke, Dr. Monroe."

But he's not joking. Jabari *is* hot. He knows it and I know it, too. I'm trying to pretend not to be intrigued or interested, though his flirting and persistence is quite flattering. But I've got young ones and a career to think about, after all. And making sure Jus and Junior get into the colleges they want. Those are my top priorities. Not love. Or a vacation lover. Or a new friendship or flirtation with my young ones' principal.

"Why me?" I go. Awkward. Showing my cards. Because I know *why me*. This drink is definitely making me loosen up. "I mean, why so soon on this trip?"

"You're right," Jabari says, putting his drink down. He stands up, the towel falls, and the yellow Speedo and all that Jabari wonderfulness in front of my eyes. "You just got here. Let's head outside. Plus, you need to get out them clothes and take a dip in the pool or the ocean just beyond the backyard."

"No, Jabari. Stay. For a minute, anyway."

"You sure?"

"Truth? Yes. Stay."

"Want some truth, Justin?" Jabari says. "I'm a little buzzed. This is all new to me, to be honest. I got divorced a couple years ago and…I'm talking too much. You're right, I'll chill."

"Now, this is how we should start a conversation and get to know each other," I say. "With some vulnerability."

"I don't know what I'm doing, really. I'm just now coming into this dating men thing at thirty-eight. Sometimes I express myself like a teenager who's trying to find himself. Your nephew, Elijah, has been a good friend and a help."

"Aww. Elijah is great, for the most part," I say. "I gotta admit, it's new to me, too. I'm sure Elijah's told you. Or you've googled."

"Your divorce situation?"

"Yeah."

"And figuring it all out? At this stage of life?"

"Yeah," I say. I feel tears coming on for whatever reason. Not doing this in front of a stranger. "Why am I like this? Why are you...never mind."

"I know when I'm feeling someone. Even if it's on a superficial, 'I'm his kids' principal and a new part of his nephew's crew' kinda level."

"We've got plenty of time to know each other, professionally or personally."

"I'ma hold you to that," Jabari says. "Shall we keep talking now? Or want to go join the rest of them out there?"

"Let's make a deal. Let's go spend time with Elijah and company now. But I promise we can try and get to know each other during these few days in Miami. And most definitely when we're back in L.A."

CHAPTER SEVEN

Elijah: Live in the 305!

By seven p.m., we are all ready for our evening nap.

Much of our first full day of vacation consists of drinks, herbs, food, and familiarizing ourselves with each other's Miami personas. One of my favorite things about traveling, especially with my besties, is the personas I get to try on and different ways of being. I do not recommend doing this if you're unable to imagine being different, if you're scared of what you'll find out about yourself. When I travel with Ezra especially, I tend to try being lavish and ostentatious. I try to be extra.

Uncle J finally relaxed a bit and found himself a little trip buddy with Jabari. Thank goodness. Mission accomplished. Just call me matchmaker amongst other good things.

"Okay y'all, I'm headed to my room to rest," Lenay says. "Keep it down, down here."

Lenay walks up the flight of stairs into the master bedroom. She insisted she get the master since she's paying the most for this Airbnb.

"Set your alarm for ten. We're leaving here at midnight!" Ezra yells from the kitchen island while cutting up a pineapple that will be refrigerated and eaten right before we go out into the night.

Miami nightlife doesn't start until midnight. Way different than life in L.A. Going to any club in Miami before midnight, not recommended, because you're wasting energy. A discovery from my first adult trip here five years ago. Lesson learned. Lesson applied tonight.

Right before I pass out in my queen bed, I open my phone to text Jabari and Uncle Justin to let them know we will be leaving the beach house at midnight, headed to South Beach to go to a Black/Brown gay party. I notice a missed call from a number I do not have saved. In my inebriated haze, I text Jabari and Uncle Justin in a group chat. As soon as I send the text, I kinda sober up just enough to realize I may have made a major mistake. I group chatted, which means I gave Jabari my uncle's actual number without his consent. Not his Google number, his assistant's number, not his office number, his actual personal exclusive ten-people-have-this-number number. Damnit. I pass…out.

❖

In my dream, I am on a private jet headed to a private party. I am dressed for a red carpet. At this party everyone knows my name, the award-winning Elijah Golden. When I deplane, I'm greeted with flashing lights and rose petals. At first, the flashing lights are cute. A flash here, a flash there. The deep tinted sunglasses I am wearing help. But as I walk down the red carpet, the lights become more and more intense, and the red path becomes harder to follow. Flash. Flash. Flash-flash-flash-flash. I try to ask for the flashing to stop, but it intensifies. I feel myself falling—perhaps I was tripped—and before I hit the ground face first, someone catches me. I look up to see whose arms catch my fall, then my alarm wakes me.

❖

The first night on a vacation is never the best night out, but in this case, it's the only night we actually go out partying together. I should have known something was off when I woke up from the falling dream, or when Uncle J never responded to my text updating him about our night plan.

When the driver calls and says he'll be here in five minutes, Lenay yells for us to meet in the kitchen for a shot and pump of energy powder, aka cocaine. No one in my crew really uses drugs outside of marijuana and alcohol, so we all laugh as we make our way to gather around the kitchen island. To our surprise, Lenay has six full shot glasses lined up and three small lines of white powder ready.

"I know you lying." Ezra laughs as they take out the pineapple they chopped and chilled in the refrigerator.

"What? Two shots each!" Lenay laughs, avoiding the obvious objection to the three lines of damn coke.

I side-eye Lenay and take a piece of pineapple.

"Come on! We are in Miami! Let's get loose. No one will judge you."

Lenay hands us our first round of shots.

It's moments like this that I remember Lenay is half white and grew up with white people. Still parties with them.

"How did you even travel with it?" I say.

"Salud!" we say in unison. We drink our first shot.

"I have my ways," Lenay says and passes our final shot. "Hurry up, the driver is almost here."

I've never done coke before, but I'm a bit curious as to what it feels like. With each new or different experience, I tell myself it'll help expand me as an actor. But hard drugs are something else. Before I decide if I'll join in the coke-tivities, Lenay seems to notice I'm on the verge of saying no. She says, "No pressure. It'll mellow you out anyway, you've been drinking all day."

She leans down, sniffs her line. Afterward, Ezra says, "Fuck it. Take me back to college." Then snorts the line.

Then I'm left there. Contemplating.

"You sure it'll mellow me out?"

"Most likely," Ezra says. "It's a balancer with alcohol."

I lean down and look at the last line of energy powder left. What the hell. They got my back if anything happens. I mimic their movements, closing one nostril and inhaling with the free nostril.

They both cheer.

There's a rush. I shake my head.

Then we are out of the door and into the car.

Then we are in the middle of the dance floor.

My shirt is off, and Ezra is dancing on someone.

Then Lenay is no longer dancing right beside me.

It's all snapshots. And tequila shots. I'm dripping with sweat.

I walk to the outside area to look for Lenay, but really I need to cool off.

"You're an actor, aren't you? I've seen you in something," a blurry face says while approaching me.

Once directly in my face, the face is handsome. A warm cinnamon brown, full lips, and doe-eyed. We are the same height. Five-ten. But in Hollywood, on paper, I'm six feet tall. The two extra inches mean something.

"No, you haven't," I say, flattered someone outside of L.A.'s struggling creative scene has noticed me. In Miami, of all places.

"Sure I have," he says while smiling. There's a gold trim

around a few of his bottom teeth. He's really handsome. But not from L.A. type of handsome. "I've seen you in a few commercials," he says, all Miami cool and smooth.

Yup, he's caught me. I've done Foot Locker, Taco Bell, Colgate, a No Tobacco campaign, and a PrEP commercial. You'd think I'd be on my way to an Academy Award by now.

I laugh.

"I'm Elijah Golden," I say, not sure why I gave him my whole name. I usually tell strangers to just call me E.

"I'm Rojo," he says.

Rojo, red? Then I notice under the dim patio lights, his curly hair is a reddish brown color. Natural redhead. A Black redhead.

"Do the curtains match the carpet?" I think I'm thinking it, but I'm actually saying it. I am clearly high.

"Wow," he says, as if he's surprised or insulted. He sounds intrigued. Fuck, who am I? I laugh it off because I'm so lost right now. "You wanna find out?"

"I do." I'm thinking, but I'm saying again.

Then without missing a beat, he unzips his pants and pulls out a semi-erect penis. No underwear. What in the Miami is going on? However, I notice the pubic hair color indeed matches his head hair.

I am mesmerized. Stunned. Stuck. My mouth agape and wet.

"You like that, huh?" he says, flopping his chubby back into his trousers.

I slowly nod, signaling I in fact do like that.

Like a rabbit out of a hat, Lenay appears and starts asking what the hell am I doing, what would Zaire think? How about what the hell was *she* thinking, getting me to try something stronger than weed? I try to tell her I haven't a clue what's going on, but nothing comes out. I try introducing her to my new associate, Rojo-Red, but she pulls me away. I hear Rojo laughing and tells me he'll catch me later. I wonder if he means it, because I want him to mean it. So I say, "I hope so."

Then I'm back in a moving machine with wheels.

Then I'm on a soft cushiony thing.

Then I'm asleep.

❖

The next couple of days Uncle J is a bit quiet and unresponsive with my solo texts. He and Jabari send group chats, surprisingly, as they enjoy random spots and eateries in South Florida. I am now certain Uncle J has found his piece of peace on this Miami trip.

Meanwhile, Ezra, Lenay, and I are still in the beachfront Airbnb, floating around zombie-like. We definitely went too hard on night one. We make it out of the house only to enjoy the pool. We have all of our snacks and meals delivered. Technology for the win.

We spend the next two days simply enjoying each other's company. On our final night, instead of ordering out, we decide to have groceries delivered to prepare dinner together. There's something special about the process of making a meal with and for the ones you love. After dinner, Ezra insists we play this questions game.

We are sitting in the living room, and they bring out a deck of cards with intimate questions.

"Let's play a game," Ezra says as they shuffle the cards. "Take it a little slower and deeper on our last night."

I've known Ezra since we were teens. They've been my best friend since our sophomore year of high school. We've had so many important life shifts together. In every major life event, Ezra has been there with me and I with Ezra. The parties, funerals, the breakups, the moves. We hold each other's deepest or most embarrassing secrets. Then, in college, we met Lenay. She was discreetly messing around with a girl Ezra was friends with. But when Lenay and the girl finally called it quits, we found ourselves more fond of Lenay. Sometimes, relationships be that way. Nearly a decade out of college, the three of us have witnessed each other expand into the people we are today.

Ezra explains the rules. Each person pulls a card and reads it to the person on their left. The person on the left has to follow the instruction by responding to the question or statement on the card. Simple enough. I find myself a bit anxious, curious as to how much more could I actually learn about the both of them, Ezra especially.

"I'll read first," Ezra says, then flips over the card at the top of the deck.

Lenay and I are both eager to know what's on the card, although Lenay is the one to respond because she is on Ezra's left side.

"New rule!" Ezra laughs.

Of course. Just like Ezra, always making up new rules whenever they feel like it, whenever it feels right.

"We all have to answer this one to each other," Ezra states.

"Uh-oh," Lenay says, "What are you about to ask?"

Ezra looks at us with a sweet smile and a glaze in their eyes and begins to read the card.

"Talk about the time you first knew you loved me. Start your statement with *I knew I loved you when.*"

Out of all the things I know about the both of them, out of all the things they know about me, this question of when I knew I loved them, and when they loved me, is a reflection I am grateful to be able to explore, right here, right now, in this moment. Sober.

LEIMERT PARK, LOS ANGELES

77° | Humidity 52%

Project List

- When is Jeanine planning to see Justin and Justice?—personal, Jeanine
- Research diets/practitioners that reduce risk of colon cancer, heart disease, other aging problems—personal
- Sonoma—personal, Trevor
- Who is Jabari; background—personal, Elijah
- Holidays and hosting. Sacramento/L.A.—personal, parents, maybe Brenda
- Benefits of pre-paying college tuition—Felicia
- Is the Ojai place underutilized? Do we need it?—Felicia
- Background check future interns working with me—NABJ friends, Alumni Association
- Do Justin & Justice need cars at college?—Elijah, Justin/Justice
- Change phone numbers and emails—again—personal
- Why aren't people including Black identity in immigration narrative?; possible story—personal; contacts
- Elijah's finances—personal; Elijah
- Look into therapy for just me (not Justin & Justice); can I trust a therapist with my life and privacy?—personal
- Who do Justin and Justice like, date, want to date?—personal, Elijah, Jeanine
- ~~Vacation?~~
- Contacts for Elijah's acting work—personal; contacts
- Do I have enough to live without working?—personal; Felicia

CHAPTER EIGHT

Justin: It's Scheduled

It's Elijah's and my first time seeing each other in person since the Miami trip.

When I have time on Sunday mornings, my nephew and I meet up unless my young ones are home for the weekend. They're still on the East Coast with their grandparents, and that's perfect for me because I have a few things on my mind about Miami that I need to discuss with him.

Our ritual. First, I drive all the way from my place in Ladera Heights and pick up Elijah at his apartment in K-Town right before seven. He usually brings one of his kombucha drinks, which I really can't stand the taste or smell of, and then he syncs one of his meditation apps to my truck's sound system to help us center ourselves while I drive us over to the Leimert Park farmers market.

There, we help two Black LGBTQ neighborhood organizations Elijah connected me to—LADS and In The Meantime—by bagging or boxing up bruised but edible fruits and vegetables for food-insecure families, seniors, and youth. After, we do a little shopping for our own fresh produce for the week. And I sign a few autographs and take a few photos with the Black grandmas who recognize me as the *More at Four/Live at Five* guy. It's fun. Then we go our separate ways by ten or eleven. For me, that usually involves some Sunday afternoon activity with my young ones if they're home. For Elijah, it involves one of the million jobs he does to sustain himself, jobs which he could easily give up and work full-time with and for me and the twins in between his nonexistent acting gigs.

But before we begin today, just as he gets in my truck, I go, "Well, look at you, Elijah Golden."

"Good morning, Uncle J," he says. He's got on some oversized black celebrity sunglasses, a baseball cap, and EarPods, like he doesn't want to engage with me or anyone else this morning. Surprised he heard me call out his name.

"So, I get the first and last name treatment this morning," he says and smiles, taking a pod out of his left ear. "What's got you all pressed this morning?"

"I'm not pressed." I put the car in drive as soon as Elijah's buckled in and got that kombucha situated in the center console. "I'm disappointed in you, nephew."

"I knew that's why I hadn't heard from you these past few days," Elijah says. "The coke incident. Miami. I'm disappointed in me, too."

"Are you really?" I say, as I make a left from Olympic Boulevard onto Arlington Avenue. The straight shot route on the streets, no freeways, will make for easy conversation and a no-stress drive for me. Easy for conversation, since, as my young ones like to say, I'm no good at multitasking while driving.

"Yeah, I am," he says. "I told Lenay and Ezra that's not my thing, but they were all like, 'don't kill the vacation vibe, Elijah,' so I didn't kill the vibe."

"You're a grown man, Elijah."

"I know I'm grown, Uncle J," Elijah repeats after me, with what sounds like a hint of sarcasm or annoyance. I hope

I'm wrong. I don't want to argue. Just get a point across, then move on.

"I'd expect Jus and Junior to fall for peer pressure, but not you, Elijah. I didn't let you come to L.A. just so you can be a fuck-up, nephew. I've worked too hard to support you and everyone else in the family so you don't have to be average and do mediocre things. I mean, do you really know your little friends?"

"I hope you don't talk like this to my cousins when you're disappointed," Elijah says, syncing his device to my truck. Calming nature sounds fill the cab. It's not my thing, but I do appreciate these moments of calm with Elijah. Much different than my typical on-the-go, always-doing-something life. "We all went to college together, by the way, in case you forgot."

"You're funny," I say, referring to Elijah's meditation app. "I get your point, Elijah. I didn't mean to go zero to a hundred on you...or your friends."

"Thanks. Point taken. And I didn't need this first thing in the morning on our uncle-nephew day together."

"Apologies."

"And I'm done with experimenting. It was just for the trip. Seriously."

"You're lucky I didn't call Brenda or your grandma and tell her what I saw and heard in Miami," I say. "We don't need Brenda's dramatics, though, and you know what I'm talking about. And with that, I am done preaching this morning. But I don't condone. Remember that."

"Thank you, Uncle J," he says as he puts the cap back on his kombucha, which he's barely touched on the drive over. "I do have a question, though. Have you ever had sex with a friend of someone you're dating or have dated?"

"Say it again?" I'm not hard of hearing, but I just need to

make sure I heard Elijah correctly the first time. Sometimes, he can be all over the place. Like he is now. "I'm confused."

"Let me rephrase it," Elijah says. "Sex with a friend of your partner."

"I'm still confused. But I mean, I'd have to dig back in the crates of undergrad or my doctoral program, from way before Jeanine."

"I mean now."

"I'm not dating anyone now. And I was completely loyal to Jeanine during our marriage, arrangement and all, if that's what you're talking about."

"That's not what I'm talking about, Uncle J." Elijah sighs, and I can tell he's trying to figure out how to help me understand. I think he can be overly dramatic in his head. "Soooo, let's say…"

"Or you could just tell me the story. The who, what, where, when, how of it. We have a schedule and can't keep the volunteer work waiting."

"Oh yeah, that. I can just do that."

"Thank you."

"Long story short." Elijah takes a deep breath.

"Oh Lord," I say as we stop at a red light near Exposition Boulevard. Means we're also nearing the end of our drive to Leimert Park. "What now, Elijah?"

"I may or may not have had sex with Zaire's best friend before I knew Zaire. Lenay thinks the reason I don't want to move in with Zaire is because I have this secret. I have yet to tell Zaire I had sex with his bestie *before* I knew him. Ezra thinks I should tell him because secrets about sex always come out and it can damage good things. What do you think? Have you had an experience like that? Light's green!" Elijah speeds out, slurring many of his words together.

My nephew is carrying so much right now. Lord knows

we haven't had time to catch up and talk about our lives on a personal note in a while. That definitely didn't happen in Miami. So, before I give my sex and relationships therapist advice, or lack thereof, I go back to the cohabitation conversation Elijah and I just had.

"I think it's common for people to have slept with someone in their friend or dating circle…and living together is a big transition," I say, multitasking conversation topics. "Has Zaire really talked to you about living together?"

"Has he!" Elijah scoffs. "It's all he hints, breathes, texts, and talks about. He has even started saying *when* we move in, not *if* we move in."

I've always liked Elijah's and Zaire's relationship. Zaire's the best of the list of boyfriends my nephew's brought around. I'm happily jealous of Elijah and Zaire. I sometimes wonder what my life would have been had I found a good match when I was Elijah's age. Jeanine and I had a good relationship. We respected each other more than loved. But respect is a form of love, I guess. No need to ponder on yesteryears and days gone by. Today is what matters.

"I think you and Zaire are lovely together, and you see each other so much, you practically live together now. But it doesn't matter what I think. What are your honest thoughts about it?"

Listening to Elijah share his fears warms my heart. He is like a bonus child of mine. I remember when he was born. My sister Brenda and his dad Gabriel were nervous and excited about having a child. Back then, Brenda and I were much closer. She's ten years my senior, so she had a lot of influence in my life. Which is similar to the way I have influence on the life of her son, my nephew, Elijah.

Elijah and I became closer as he got older. When he came out as queer in his teenage years, I was the person he wanted to spend most of his time with. He'd come stay with me and Jeanine and the twins in L.A. during his school breaks, which didn't always please Brenda. Through those visits, Elijah and I found we had many things in common, much more than his parents, I think, and he would always say how safe he felt around me.

So, when he comes to talk to me now, I'm sure he's not seeking advice from his parents. I always take that into consideration before I share. I do more editing to make sure I am supporting, relating, and guiding. Like I try to do with the twins.

I think Elijah's qualms are valid. Compromising. Negotiating space. All that time together. There's a lot to be certain of. And he's not yet established in his acting career, which is what brought him to L.A. from Sacramento a little over a decade ago, in addition to college. I tell him to do what he knows is right for him. I tell my young ones the same thing. When it comes to their lives, do what they want to do. I tell them to try to silence the voices of others about the things that bring them peace and joy.

Now, the other topic of the day—sex with a friend of your partner. Lord knows I do not have any expertise in that arena.

"I've never had sex with a friend of my partner," I say. "And I only had Jeanine. And I never did anything outside our marriage. Even when I wanted to."

"Right!" Elijah says in a way that feels like he's really saying *of course you haven't!* and looks out the passenger window. Maybe he's depleted. I don't know.

To show him I'm relatable and not perfect, I share my long-standing crush on Trevor. I tell him this because I need to tell someone, and I figure he needs to know my life isn't all that together.

"What!" Elijah gasps and looks at me. I've caught his attention. "Your best friend, Trevor?"

"That's the one."

"Uncle J, that's perfect," he says. "When are you going to tell him? Wait, what about Jabari? And whatever y'all did in Miami?"

"I didn't do anything with Jabari but eat and drink and let him crash in my suite. Three-month rule, you know. Plus he works with Jus and Junior, and they don't like him. Or, rather, they don't like the school anymore."

"Three-month rule? You ain't dating no one to have a three-month rule, Uncle J."

"You know what I mean, Elijah," I say. "Jabari is just a... friend of yours."

"He's so into you, though, Uncle J. Look at you pulling in the men in your forties, fifties, sixties," Elijah says while snapping his fingers with each decade.

He thinks he's funny. I zing him back.

"Remind me again when you're going to tell Zaire about sleeping with his friend?"

"Wooooow." Elijah laughs. "When you go low..."

"Hey, you asked me," I say. "But anyway. Do you think I should say something to Trevor?"

"Of course! I think you and Trevor would make a great couple. I think you and Jabari would make a great couple."

I always wonder what people mean when they say things like that. Sure, Trevor and I would look cute together. Distinguished. Successful. Charming. Black men together. On red carpets. In magazines. On vacations. But so would Jabari and I. He's attractive, well educated, and interested in me, for sure, but a little on the aggressive and needy side. But that body erases quite a few doubts.

Here I go daydreaming while driving. And like that, arriving in Leimert Park.

I park the truck in the spot reserved for me near the market. Before we get out, I tell Elijah I think he should explain everything to Zaire. All at once. But only when he feels ready.

Then as we are walking across the street to meet the staff from In The Meantime and LADS, my phone rings. It's Trevor.

"Trevor. What's up?"

"Don't cross the street without me," Trevor says. "I'm parking right now."

I look behind me and there he is, getting out of his Tesla. I hang up the phone and suddenly I'm nervous. Trevor. My crush. My best friend.

"Apparently, we have a party crasher," I say to Elijah. "Trevor is joining us."

Moments before Trevor makes it to us, Elijah repeats the advice I gave to him earlier, but with a slight twist.

"Tell Trevor you like him," he says and pauses. "But not when you're ready. More when it feels right."

"Right. Thanks," I say and chuckle.

CHAPTER NINE

Justin: Or Better Late Than...

"Well, this has been fun," I say as Trevor and I set our napkins on the table. "A nice surprise. Thank you."

We are finishing up our lunch at Trevor's favorite Ethiopian restaurant, Merkato on Fairfax, and the server has just left the bill. After Trevor popped up unexpectedly at our day of service in Leimert Park, he asked if I wanted to extend our friend-date for a couple hours. With my young ones heading back in a couple days and no real schedule ahead of me for this day, I said yes. Who can pass up stewed meats, injera, honey wine, and time with my best friend and crush on a Sunday afternoon?

"Thank you for indulging me, Justin," Trevor says. "I wouldn't want to be with anyone else right now."

"Oh, please. I'm sure you wanted to be with your little friend Sonoma today, right?"

"I'm here because I want to be here." Trevor rolls his eyes and then goes, "Besides, I need someone a little more...I don't know."

He stares at me. And I wonder if this is the time when Trevor will confess his unyielding love and devotion to me after all these years. Or if this is the moment when it feels right, as my nephew Elijah encouraged earlier, and I say what's on my heart. That I want Trevor.

"Say it, Trevor." I lean in with eye contact and attention. "Say what's on your heart."

"I don't know." Trevor grabs my hand. "You sure you're ready for this?"

"Of course." I'm getting warm inside, a combination of honey wine and what I hope will be the beginning of something special with Trevor. "You know you can tell me anything."

"Well, this feels so shallow after all you've told me about your job, Elijah and Miami, and what's on your mind about Jus and Junior."

"Shallow? You? Trevor Smith? No way."

We both laugh because we know it's true. Trevor can be a little on the shallow side, while I've always been the serious one. I realize we haven't let go of our hands across the table. That's not so shallow.

"Okay, here goes," Trevor says. He lets go of my hands and crosses his arms. Then he starts flailing and goes, "I need someone a little more oral, if you know what I mean."

The last thing I want to know about is Trevor's sex life with Sonoma. I don't want to know Trevor is having sex, even though I know he's having sex. I just want him to want it with me. But I indulge the conversation.

"What do you mean, Trevor?"

"He doesn't suck." Trevor reaches for the glass in front of him, downing the small splash of honey wine left. "He doesn't do head. He doesn't eat. He doesn't do any of that. But he's ready, willing, and eager for me to do any and all of the above for him. Which I don't mind, because you've seen Sonoma, and he's just edible in every way. I mean EVERY way. I've got dozens of his throat babies that I haven't even named yet. Still..."

Info I didn't ask for. But anyway, any unscrupulous friend, or an acquaintance with questionable motives, would see this as a way in. I'm not that type.

"Wow, that's unfortunate," is all I can muster.

"Yeah. See. Shallow. I know you've got lots on your mind besides my sex life...or lack thereof...though I gets mine and get him his, if you know what I mean."

Ugh. Details I don't want to know. I just want Trevor. And if he's ever fortunate to experience me, he'll know I will do anything and everything he claims Sonoma doesn't do. But the timing. Always the timing.

"Well, yes, I do have a lot on my mind," I say. "But you're my longest-lasting and best friend. I'm open to talk whenever you want."

My phone buzzes. A text from an 818 number that I don't recognize.

"You're busy, Justin," Trevor says. "We can connect later when we're both home. I'm going to Sonoma's apartment after this. Give him some before he leaves for a six-week shoot in Atlanta tomorrow morning. I think it's six weeks. Or maybe I'm thinking about that almost six-inch girth. Mmm. Exaggerating. But still, close enough."

Details I don't want to know from Trevor. Again.

I tap my phone and open the 818. It's Jabari. I forgot Elijah mistakenly put my real number in a group chat in Miami, so now Jabari has my personal number.

Thinking of you and the Miami trip. Wanna keep up the momentum. Busy today?

I smile. Not that I'd forgotten about Jabari and Miami, but being around Trevor, being demoted at the station, being

worried about Jabari coming on too strong, blah blah blah...
Jabari hasn't exactly been on the top of my to-do list.

"What you smiling about, Justin?" Trevor asks.

"Really...nothing," I say, reaching for the lunch bill after
I set my phone down. "I've got it."

"Nah, *friend*." Trevor pulls the check away from me.
"You're the one about to take a huge pay cut. I got this."

"Thanks, friend." And put myself back in reality. Trevor
and I are friends. Best friends. Nothing else.

As Trevor hands over his card and the bill to the server,
I pick up the phone and do something I haven't done in a
long time. Definitely not since I started dating Jeanine back
in the day. And since Trevor isn't giving me the time of day,
romantically, as I want, I text Jabari back.

Not too busy for you.

❖

I probably shouldn't have been so quick to respond to
Jabari's text on my private number. I probably shouldn't have
invited him over for keeping up the momentum of Miami. I
probably shouldn't have Marvin Gaye's *I Want You* album
playing on every Sonos speaker in each room of the house and
in the backyard, too.

But I do. And I am waiting for Jabari to arrive. He promised
punctuality and timed the trip from his place in Altadena to
mine in Ladera Heights to arrive by five. Figured that's early
enough to enjoy some daylight hours in the backyard, and
not too late to imply an overnight invitation. Not that I'd rule
against an overnight visit, but I don't know Jabari like that,
and it's been a little too long since I've been with anyone
intimately, let alone another man. I wouldn't even know what

to do. Am I even attractive? What does one do when sleeping with someone new? Do people sleep together on a first date?

Getting ahead of myself. Way too ahead. My mind stays busy.

From the guesthouse fridge, I grab the charcuterie board I ordered earlier today from Oak & Honey and set it up on the backyard table. Nearby, I've got a stainless steel wine chiller with two bottles of McBride Sisters' Sparkling Brut on ice. I hope he likes the wine choice, from a winery owned by Black women. The portable heaters surrounding the outdoor seating area are on low right now, because I know the temperature will drop as the sun sets. Not that we're going to be having a late night date or anything.

Like clockwork, Jabari texts his arrival, and I do a once-over of the backyard seating area where we'll be. I'm getting butterflies and wonder if I'm dressed okay in some basic dark denim and a cream sweater just in case it gets chilly. Trying to look neat, but not too dad-chic for this date or whatever with Jabari. I open up the fence connecting the backyard and driveway, where he's parked his SUV behind mine. The symbolism. Ha.

"Hey there," Jabari says as he's getting out the front driver's seat and waves my way. "Be right there, gotta grab something out the back."

"I can help, if you want," I say and head out to the driveway to meet and greet.

"I got it, but if you want."

He's wearing his signature color, a yellow V-neck light knit sweater and some lime green pants. Jabari hugs me, and he smells oh-so-sweet-and-manly, and I'm like fuckfuckfuckfuck. His scent is gonna get me on the first date alone. With no nephew, friends, or young ones around.

"Hey."

"Hey," he says, looking in my eyes, not pulling away. "You look good."

"You look good."

"I brought some things for our get-together," he says "They're in the back seat. Good to see you again, Justin."

He smiles. I smile back. *This is an actual date with a grown man. Don't mess it up, Justin.*

"Good to see you, too," I say instead and smile. "And I promise, no arguments, no conflicts, no drama. Like Miami."

"Did we have arguments, conflicts, or drama in Miami?" Jabari asks. "Other than you not letting me…never mind. Or was that your way of saying, 'I like you, but let's feel each other out?'"

"You think I like someone here?" I pull away from the hug before this turns into second or third base in the driveway. Those eyes. That smile. That body. Fuckfuckfuckfuck.

"You wouldn't have invited me to your house if you didn't." Jabari pulls out a gift bag for wine and a decent-sized bouquet of colorful flowers from the back seat of his truck. I've never seen a yellow leather interior in a truck before, but it's tasteful and really elegant. So are the flowers. This man. "I know you just don't let anyone in your circle or space."

"Okay, you got me, and my nephew talks too much." I take the flowers from Jabari so he can close and lock his truck. "Let's head to the backyard before some nosy neighbor or paparazzi wonders who's the hottie Justin Monroe's got at his house."

"Oh, I get backyard action," Jabari says and laughs. "You really are going to keep this PG-13, huh?"

"That's to be seen, Jabari. Depends on if you're a good boy or not."

On the way to the backyard, Jabari takes my hand into

his. He squeezes it and feels warm, and all of a sudden I've got the first-date giddiness I felt back in the day when I first met and asked Jeanine out for a date in college. Not that this night with charcuterie and wine in L.A. is the same as pizza and beer dating in a Midwestern college town. I can't believe it's been that long since my last first date. I can't believe this is my first date since Jeanine and I decided to part ways and be as happy and Black and free and queer as we always knew we were.

"This is nice," Jabari says, looking around. "Look at you, Justin Monroe."

"Thanks. It's just a house. It's just a backyard," I say, downplaying the years of work and perfection turning this house into a mini-mansion.

"So modest. That's a trait I admire. You've done so much, yet you're so humble."

"If only you heard the egomaniacal thoughts in my head. I try not to let my job and being known by the public get to me. I'm just a Black boy from small-town Sacramento."

"Elijah's shared."

"Elijah talks too much about my business, but that's family."

"Family is important," Jabari says. "Which is what built up my nerve to text you about keeping up the momentum of Miami."

"I was wondering why I'd get an out-of-the-blue text from you on a random Sunday. I thought I put up too many road blocks."

"Well, I mean you didn't give me any in Miami."

"Wasn't in the plan to give you some."

"Touché," Jabari says. "But truth. I took my mom to church today, and the word got to me. Something about not being anxious, praying about your wants and desires. And I thought about you, Justin, and decided to text when I dropped Mom off. Hope that's not weirding you out."

"I think it's beautiful you and your mom go to church together."

"Not every Sunday," he says and laughs. "I'm not one of those God-squad folks."

"Thank God—no pun intended. You won't believe the hypocritical hate emails I get from them because of my commentaries and reporting, and just for being Black these days."

"No worries. Just special occasions. And mostly when I'm on summer break and have a little more free time. A brotha be busy. I know you know about busy."

"Yes, I have a busy and full life, Jabari," I say. I'm also making a mental note to talk with my nephew again about what he shares and doesn't share about my life. "And here we are, finding time to meet up again. Welcome to my place."

"How'd you know this is one of my favorite albums of all time?" Jabari says when we get to the seating area where I've set up the charcuterie and wine. I'd forgotten I'd left the speakers and Marvin Gaye on rotation this evening. Jabari sets his wine bag and the flowers I'm carrying down. "Dance first?"

So many firsts. Among them, being pulled into a man's arms and being serenaded with Jabari's on-pitch singing to Marvin's song "After the Dance" on my backyard patio. I feel goosebumps as his hands grasp my waist and squeeze gently. We find a slow dance rhythm that works for us, though the song is more suitable for the Midwestern ballroom stepping style of dance I've seen some of my older relatives do at family gatherings. I put my arms around his shoulders and lean in, feeling the firmness of his chest, back, and abs against mine. His scent, which I cannot identify, is driving me crazy. This is nice. This is weird. This is romantic. I'm floating, and we haven't even had a glass of wine yet. It's just after five in the evening, much too early to be thinking what I'm thinking.

"Thanks for obliging me, Justin," Jabari says, letting go. "Let's crack open some wine and this charcuterie. Another fave of mine. I swear you're reading my mind."

"Maybe it's my nephew, Elijah. Just joking. I just wanted to keep it simple. As we keep up the momentum, as you say."

"I'm down for white or red," Jabari says. "Whatever feels right for you and for us right now."

I decide to open the red Jabari brought over, so he gets to make a contribution to our first date.

Over a couple bottles of wine, a playlist change to some R&B slow jams we grew up with, and the landscape and outdoor lights turning on after sunset, Jabari and I ease into conversation and find many similarities in our lives, including the ones that bond us the most. He tells me more about the recent divorce that he hinted at when we were together in Miami. He's also a parent, though his daughter, a college sophomore at Howard, is a few years older than my twins. Our young ones, our love for them and their mothers, and navigating singlehood at this stage in our lives is comforting to me.

"At some point," I say as I place a couple of bottles of sparkling water in front of us, "we're going to have to talk about my young ones, your role at their school, some of the issues they're having there…and this."

I point to him. Then me. Then him again.

Jabari points to me. Then him. Then me again. "This is a this?"

"It might be. I know we haven't spent a lot of time together, and we're still getting to know each other, but I'm willing."

We stare at the flames in the fire pit. By now, we're sitting next to each other. He pulls my hand into his.

"You're really handsome, Justin."

And before I can respond, Jabari's lips are pressed against mine, and I'm feeling softness, warmth, and fireworks all at the same time. I let go and open my mouth to receive more of Jabari's affection. Though it feels no different, physically, than kissing my ex-wife, it feels different emotionally. Like this is who and what I should have been all my life, had I had the courage to be myself, to not follow a life script, to not worry about what the industry or viewers or fans or some family would think. Like this is what life could have been for Jeanine and for me. Free.

I know it's weird to say I feel human now. That I'm not just the *More at Four* or *Live at Five* guy. That I'm not just the one who keeps multiple family members afloat. That I'm not just a single dad, though successful fatherhood is my primary goal. That I'm not just the journalist with a doctorate trying to stay number one in the ratings. That I'm more than the one who's being demoted to weekend newscasts. That I'm more than the hate a bunch of fake-news fanatics and low-information viewers like to spew on me, which is part of the reason why I keep my young ones in a private boarding school in Burbank most of the week. That I'm more than Justin Monroe who has a crush on his best friend and next door neighbor, Trevor Smith.

Shit. Trevor.

I pull away from Jabari just as I feel a hint of his tongue dancing against mine.

"What happened?" Jabari asks.

"Nothing. I'm just overthinking."

"Overthinking what?"

"Never mind," I say. But I'm thinking about twenty-plus years of crush and feelings for Trevor. "You're a good kisser, Jabari. I wasn't expecting that. I wasn't expecting this..."

I point at myself. Then to Jabari. Then to me again.

"This is a this? We're a this?"

"I'm thinking."

"Don't think," Jabari says. "Feel."

"I don't have as much experience with all this as you do. No judgment on you and what you said you did while married, Jabari, but I stayed loyal to Jeanine all of the years of our marriage. This is new for me."

"I don't feel judged." He caresses the side of my face and kisses my forehead. "Having feelings is new for me. Everything and everyone else was just...sex."

"I wasn't born yesterday."

We laugh.

"You're a good kisser, too, by the way," Jabari says. "Like you've been kissing men all your life. Someone taught you."

"This journalist watches lots of videos, if you know what I mean."

Jabari puts his hand around my neck and pulls me in for what I know will be another round of kissing.

"This is a this," Jabari says. "This ain't no video."

After another ten minute round of enjoying each other's kisses, I pull away and smile.

I don't know if it's the wine or the makeout session that's got me feeling all woozy, but I let go of non-disclosure agreements, background checks, and the guilt I carry of having needs and having them met by someone else other than me. "I know you've got a light work week with your remaining break, and I'm off for a few days before my young ones are back in town. But if you'd like to see the inside of the house tonight, you're more than welcome."

This is how I wish we'd started in Miami. But better late than never.

Chapter Ten

Justin: And So It Goes...

"...and so it goes, L.A. I'll see you next weekend. Take care and thanks for tuning in on this Sunday night. Do good. And make it a great week for everyone in your world."

I smile. Wait for the director to motion that we're off the air. And smile disappears.

I'm only doing these weekend newscasts until my contract ends right after the November election. Just long enough to earn my final bit of salary, stock options, and other benefits so I can make sure Jus and Junior are secure in the college of their choice, which, if I placed my chips all on black, is most likely going to be an HBCU somewhere.

Jus and Junior took the news surprisingly well, in that way teenagers tell you they're concerned, but they're also centered on their own well-being. I thought it would go awry, but keeping with my promise to deal honestly with my young ones, I told them in a straightforward way.

"Your father is being demoted at the station," I said as we sat around the dining room table the evening Jus and Junior returned from Brooklyn and the HBCU tour with their grandparents. "I'll be working weekends only starting in a couple weeks when the fall season begins."

"Like no Monday to Friday work anymore?" Junior asked. "If the same take-home pay, then score."

"We don't have to worry about money right now, you all. Only change might be our schedules. Like, if you leave the Hills on weekends to come home, you'll be here alone."

"Bet," Junior said, winking across the table at his sister. "Parties. I mean friend gatherings. Just joking."

"With your cousin Elijah supervising," I said. "I'll see if we can get him to give up one of his weekend jobs to spend time with you on the weekends you decide to come home."

We passed around the bags of In-N-Out burgers Jus and Junior wanted when they landed at LAX. So much for my diet and eating plan and enjoying real food with my young ones. Now that I'd be shifting from the pace of Monday to Friday newscasts to weekends, when fewer people watched, I'd be able to indulge in everything the station's image consultants drilled in me and all the on-air talent to avoid. Mainly food. In portions I wanted.

"I have a question for you, Dad," Jus said while dipping a fry in her strawberry shake. "You will have enough for us to still go to college, right? Because if you don't, we can choose something local or even a junior college."

"Jus, chill," Junior said. "We good. College is cheaper than the Hills. We good, right?"

"Of course we're good," I said. "I will always take care of you. And so will your mother. And so will your grandparents. All you both have to do is study, get good grades, and live your fullest, funnest Black lives."

"Bet," Junior said and put his EarPods in, more interested in listening to the new playlist of 80s and 90s conscious rap he curated. "Aye, can Caleb come over tonight? He got some new music to share, and it's not the same online."

"You mean your boyfriend, Caleb," Jus said, ducking out of the way of a napkin Junior threw her way. "JK, brother."

"Yes, Caleb can come over. Jus, leave your brother alone. His friend-dating-whatever life is his business."

"Sorry, brother," Jus said. She dipped another fry in her shake and then turned her attention my way. "Besides the job news, any good news, Dad?"

There is good news. Jabari. I'd wanted to wait until I got an idea if Jabari and I would be going anywhere beyond the night we spent together before I had that convo with Jus and Junior. I am not about to be one of those single parents putting their needs above their children and introducing random new dates in my young ones' lives. After just a couple dates and sleepovers, it wasn't time to just break out, "Hey Jus and Junior, your principal and I have been…"

So I deflected.

"Nothing major," I said. "If something comes up, you two will be the first to know."

"Dad's a Carlton," Junior said, despite having his EarPods in. "Ain't nothing going on with him."

And with Junior's equating me to everybody's favorite nerd from *The Fresh Prince*, I knew we'd be good in the Monroe household. At least about our family unit and about my job. Next, I'd be talking with the Sacramento family about my career's next steps, but I'd cross that bridge when needed. Not like they were keeping tabs on L.A. newscasts from northern California.

Director shouts, "That's a wrap. Time for the post-show meeting."

Though I've gotten to working the weekend newscasts, I haven't gotten used to my performance being critiqued by the newbies who've been hired by the new station management. So as soon as 11:31 p.m. hits on Saturday and Sunday nights, I pick up my bag, which I keep sitting underneath the anchor desk, and I head out the door before the newbies try and have their little debrief sessions.

I'm not against new talent coming up in the profession behind me. We all have our era and time when we're hot and in the spotlight. I had mine as the young up-and-coming anchor when I was hired sixteen years ago to replace the legendary Arvis Jefferson, who'd been a staple in L.A. news and L.A.'s Black community since the late 70s. But I'd also paid my dues, and Arvis respected that when he gave his approval to the station's owners and viewers. Way different than being blindsided with Ke'Von Carrington replacing me as the station's lead anchor.

Most of these folks recently hired at my station are barely out of journalism school, hardly paid any dues in small-town America like real journalists are supposed to do, and don't have a brain or bit of courage to think for themselves. And I don't stay for the wrap-up meetings because I don't want someone who's not even thirty telling me to stop improvising my scripts with so-called fake news when I'm only correcting the work of news writers who'd rather copy and paste the text from the basket of deplorables rather than tell our viewers the truth.

All I know is when my contract is up next year after the next major election, I'm most likely not renewing with my current station.

I send a quick group text to my young ones that I'm heading home and I hope they have a great school week ahead at the Hills. And then, as has become our habit, I dial up Jabari, who keeps me company on the car speakerphone while I drive home.

"Hey, you," Jabari says as he picks up on the first ring. "How was work today?"

It's refreshing to have someone to ask me this question who means it and who wants to get it.

"I made it a good day," I say as I pull out the station lot. "Another Sunday night of not attending the post-show team meeting, though. What are they gonna do? Demote me again? From weekends?"

"They could."

"To what? They won't."

"Let's hope not, Justin."

"I've heard a few folks been emailing up a storm to station management about me, my shift to weekends, and being replaced by Ke'Von Carrington on weekdays. Most good… about me. The fake news followers are another story."

"I get it," Jabari says. "I'm getting it, too, from some parents and the Hills' advisory board, some saying the curriculum is too loose, liberal, revisionist. They make it hard for me to make the school more palatable and representative of our students. But anyway, won't bore you. This is our time."

"They do everything to make it hard for us as Black folks to succeed."

"Ashe."

"So, I skipped out the damn post-show meeting, like I was saying earlier. The new news director still has milk on his breath, and his mom used to work with 45, so you know where he's coming from. He has nothing to say about my work. So… here I am."

"You're so rebellious, Justin."

"I feel like rebelling and coming up your way to Altadena, but I know you've got to be up early for work."

"Bad boy." Jabari lowers his voice a bit. "I'm already

in bed and you got me tempted and excited down there just hearing your voice and thinking about you being here, but…"

"I know. I know. Up at five. Workout a half hour after that. Be at the Hills by seven."

"You know your Jabari so well. I'm impressed and flattered. You're making this hard for me."

"As I usually do." I think about all the things I'd want to do to, with, and for Jabari's body tonight. And if we were in our twenties, we might just risk it all—late night, early morning on a worknight—but we're near or in our forties, and that means making more responsible decisions, I guess. "Anyway, did you watch tonight?"

"Yes I did. You did a good job tonight. No one would be able to tell how much you dislike weekends."

"Thanks," I say as I signal right to turn on LaBrea. My young ones and Elijah would be impressed with my talking and driving at the same time. I'm working on adding music in the background, but hey, small wins. "I'm ready for my next Emmy. Anyway. How you?"

"Can't complain. Missing you. Can't wait to see you."

"Same. We'll work it out."

"That we will. No doubt."

It's been tough finding time for Jabari and me to date since I started weekends. His work is a Monday through Friday gig, my off days. When he's off, I'm at the station. The Ladera Heights and Altadena distance don't make for quick visits during the week unless I drive up to his part of town. Even then, I have to dodge questions from Jus and Junior about where I am, if they FaceTime and I'm at Jabari's place.

But for the most part, we've found a relatively new rhythm with nightly calls and FaceTimes. We find that Friday evenings, when he's done at the Hills, works for him to come my way for dinner and an overnight, and then be gone before Jus and Junior get there on Saturday mornings when they decide to come home.

I'm overthinking as usual.

"I have a question for you, Jabari," I ask as I speed south on LaBrea. No traffic. Hitting all the green lights. I'll be home in record time. Maybe time to squeeze in a video call with Jabari before his midnight bedtime. "I was wondering when and how did you...after your divorce, not while you were married and seeing men...did you introduce anyone significant to your daughter?"

"Why do you ask? What's up?"

"Because at some point, I'm going to need to figure out talking with my young ones about this..."

"We're a 'this'?"

"We're a something, Jabari." I chuckle nervously. "I hope so, anyway."

"We are, Justin. I'm just joking."

"You're so dramatic."

"I can't believe it's been a couple months already. Time flies..."

"Thanksgiving is around the corner," I say. "My family is coming down from Sacramento. I was thinking it might be good for me to include you. Unless you got plans with your mom, family, and daughter already."

"Aww, I'm flattered. I need to check in with the family first."

"Of course. No pressure."

"I know where you're going with your question," Jabari says. "About my daughter, my dating life, how I introduced significant people in my life to her. Or to my mom or my ex-wife, for that matter."

"Sorry to make it so deep before your bedtime."

"I love it. This is building relationship. But truth?"

"Always."

"I haven't," Jabari says. "She knows my sexuality is why her mom and I split. But I haven't met someone significant enough yet to introduce."

"You haven't?" *Not even me?*

"Until you, Justin."

I'm relieved. And I'm smiling ear to ear.

"Until you, too, Jabari."

"You wanna change your mind and come up to Altadena?"

"I'm almost home, but I'm tempted."

"We might need a naughty FaceTime when you get in the house."

"We might." But then I think back to why I asked the question in the first place. "If we do this Thanksgiving thing, I have to talk to Jus and Junior before that. I don't want them finding out I've been hunching their principal over turkey and dressing with the Monroe village as the audience."

Jabari laughs. "And then I'll have to talk with my work and the advisory board about us. So much to do to build a relationship. But I'm in."

"I'm in." I smile, knowing I've got lots of work ahead. "And I'm pulling up to my place now."

"Glad you made it safely, Justin. And if you don't mind, I'ma raincheck our FaceTime. I need to sleep."

"Good night. Thanks for keeping me company on the drive home."

We both *mwah* through the phone, and I hang up. My phone dings with texts I missed while driving and speaking with Jabari. I get my bag out the passenger seat and open my truck door. Trevor's frantically walking across to my driveway from his place.

"Hey, friend," Trevor says as he makes his way up to my truck. "Good show tonight. Did you get my texts?"

"Haven't checked yet. Was on the phone on the way home."

"That maaaaan?"

"Someone. Is there something urgent in those six missed texts?"

Ever since Trevor and Sonoma have gotten more serious, I've backed away, perhaps unfairly, from the best friendship thing with Trevor. Not that we're not best friends anymore. I've needed space to establish something solid with Jabari while also getting past any romantic feelings I've had for Trevor. Plus, I haven't wanted to give him any ammunition to tell my young ones about my new relationship before I get to talk to them. The whole thing has been awkward.

"Can we go inside?" Trevor asks. "Your place or mine?"

Trevor is slurring a bit and his stance is wobbly.

"Come on in mine," I say, and we walk toward my front porch and door.

Once inside, I press the security code to disarm the alarm, and we head toward the kitchen/dining area where we often have heart-to-hearts.

"I need water, Justin," Trevor says and sits down. "I've been drinking. Don't judge me. I'm okay. Not gonna puke or anything on your lovely interior decor. Justin's fancy decor."

"No judgment, *friend.*" He's definitely drunk. But no judgment. We're still friends and familiar. "Where's Sonoma?"

"There *is* no Sonoma. Not anymore."

"What? Oh no. What's going on?"

"'I shoulda known better,' to quote Monica," Trevor says. He laughs. I do, too. We both have a thing for Monica and her music. She's in our generation's musical range, so to speak. "Sonoma and I had a falling-out. Again. This time it's permanent."

"Sorry to hear. I know he's meant…something…to you."

"You're so shady. *Something.*"

"No shade meant."

"I'm not dramatic. I'm not a diva. I'm not controlling. But I say three little things to Sonoma about his career—and he asked—and he goes off about how I'm not his father, that I'm always trying to tell him what to do, how to do it, why he should do it."

Trevor? Not a diva. Not dramatic. Ha.

"So, are you sure it's over? And why would he end it because you shared your opinion that he asked for?"

"I'm done. Done. No more younger men. No more of these pretty boys, actors, models, regulars, whatevers. I'ma get off the apps, too."

"No, you're not."

"You're right. I'm not."

I look up at the clock. It's nearing half past midnight, and I'd like to get a bite to eat and some sleep, but I'd also like to listen to Trevor. "Dating at our age and with our careers…is a challenge," I say. Then I remind myself I've found someone who's not quite a challenge. "Maybe that came out wrong. I have always wanted the best for you, Trevor."

"Since those days back in our first-year dorm at Mizzou," Trevor says. "You know me so well. You're my bestie, Justin. Sorry for keeping you up so late."

"You're not keeping me up." He is, but I have no schedule. It's Monday. He's got the schedule. "But I did work all weekend. And I'm tired, but okay."

"Look at us," Trevor says. "Who'd have thought? Why haven't we?"

"Here we are." I ignore the last part of Trevor's statement. "It's late. What time are you heading in tomorrow?"

"You know what time we go in for the four and five newscasts," Trevor says. "I'll be okay and in by noon."

"Sorry about Sonoma. You deserve to be happy."

"I do," Trevor says. Then he grabs my hand. "Why haven't we?"

"Why haven't we *what*?" Ugh. Why is he asking me this now? It's a little too late for this kind of conversation, and I don't mean the hour.

Trevor points from him to me to him again. I know he's got to be kidding. At this point in our lives and friendship? After all these years of me wanting him, and then being married, and watching him and his series of dates, boyfriends, lovers, and more. And wanting to be more than best friends. And especially now that I've found something special with Jabari. The timing is just off.

"Don't play stupid, Dr. Monroe," Trevor says. "You're not dumb."

"But I'm not sure what you're saying and why you're saying it now."

"Will this help?" Trevor leans in and kisses me. A peck at first on the lips. Then a little more. I can taste what seems like multiple glasses of Pinot on his tongue. It feels…good. It feels wrong. I pull away. "Did it?"

"You're drunk," I say. "This isn't right."

"I'm drunk, yes, but I know this is right." Trevor gazes deeply into my eyes. I am almost convinced he means what he's saying. "It's always been right. For the past twenty-something years it's been right."

"Trevor, we can't. We're best friends, and—"

"And that makes it even better." He shushes me by putting

a finger on my lips, and then leans in for another kiss. "We know each other so well."

I pull away. Again.

"Trevor, no. Stop. It's late. You're drunk. Let's talk more when you're sober."

"Is it that man?" Trevor rolls his eyes.

"What man?"

"*That* man."

"We can talk when you're sober, Trevor."

"I'm not stupid," he says. "I see the truck in your driveway every Friday. And I know your nephew hasn't stepped up or upgraded his car game."

"Doesn't matter. This isn't right. Right now. I'm loyal, even if I'm..."

"We both know you've always wanted me," Trevor says. "Haven't you, Justin?"

Always an ego. But has *he* wanted me, though? I want to know. I don't think I'll get a truthful answer from him. Not now, in the state he's in. "That's not important."

"Then can you pretend that you've wanted me?" Trevor asks and leans in again. "At least for tonight? I don't want to be alone tonight."

I have wanted Trevor.

Although I've put my feelings for him on ice, I do want Trevor.

And after letting twenty-plus years of longing, friendship, and wanting each other take over, in the most special way, overnight in my bedroom, I hear a phone notification at five-thirty in the morning. It's my morning greeting from Jabari, letting me know he's up and on his way to the gym.

Guilt. Regret. Remorse.

I turn on the bedside lamp and roll over to the other side

of the bed where Trevor snored lightly most of the night when we finished showing each other how much we've wanted each other.

But no Trevor. Just a Post-it on the pillow.

Thank you. I'm sorry. My lips are sealed, friend. T.

MONDAY TO-DO

- 6 a.m.: Alarm 1
- 6:15 a.m.: For Real Wake Up Alarm
- 6:20 a.m.: Stretch & Mediate, set intentions
- 6:35 a.m.: Dress
- 6:45 a.m.: Nutrients: water, smoothie, vitamins
- 7 a.m.: Bike to gym
- 7:15 a.m.: Arrive to work, set up for class
- 7:30a.m.–8:15a.m.: Spin Class; New Week, New You
- 8:20a.m.; Text Zaire
- 8:30a.m.–9:15 a.m.: Spin Class; New Week New You
- 9:30 a.m.; Call Mom
- 10 a.m.: Grocery store run
- Bread, Kombucha, grapes, broccoli, fruit roll-ups, rice, eggs, kale, Old Bay seasoning
- 11 a.m.: Rehearse for Audition
- 1 p.m.: LEAVE THE HOUSE
- 2 p.m.: AUDITION!!
- 3 p.m.–6 p.m.: Tutoring (Canceled)
- Ask Ezra about upcoming show
- 7 p.m.: Review tutoring materials for the next day
- 8 p.m.: Review spin class music

CHAPTER ELEVEN

Elijah: The Joy

Where is the gallon of ice cream when you need it? Dairy. Cow's milk ice cream. Lactose intolerance or not, I want real Tillamook.

I dread the unsettling curiosity and angst of life post-audition. I didn't do my best. I did my best in the moment, but it doesn't feel like it was good enough.

I got through my lines and the small talk afterward. The five observers in the room were all wearing different textures of black except for the person behind the camera recording. She had on a bright red T-shirt, which is probably the reason I didn't do as well as I should have. Damn distraction. I was asked to redo the scene thrice. Each one slightly different from the last. I'm used to that request. One more urban, the next more suburban, the last take more aloof—whatever the hell that means.

I did what they asked. There were a few head nods and chuckles. There also was a tear leaving my left eye when I finished the last take. Don't know where that tear came from. Maybe it'll add to it. Maybe it won't. Soon enough Lyrique, my agent, will call asking how it went, and I'll have to figure out how honest to be with her.

Once, years ago, I took a dance class at the Debbie Allen Dance Academy, and Ms. Allen would stop mid-routine and shout, "I don't want to see the work. I want to see the joy!"

What a concept—less technicality, more joy.

I've dedicated much of my adult life working, working, working, attempting to perfect my skills and highlight my talent. Hearing Ms. Allen say, "I want to see the joy," from that day forward, I told myself I would do all things from that space—finding the joy in my work.

All week I've been rehearsing because I loved the scene I received, and I love acting, and I had an unwavering knowledge the joy would shine through. Yet I'm not so sure about the joy shining.

Perhaps when Lyrique calls, I will tell her I know I was off, or maybe I'll say what I know to be both true and safe: *What will be, will be, and I'm ready to receive what is mine.*

Ugh! I want Tillamook ice cream.

But instead of driving across town to my favorite parlor in Silverlake, I sit in my car and spend a few moments in Twitterland to escape. Twitter comes in clutch for three reasons to me. First, it makes you laugh with all the ridiculousness. Black Twitter is unmatched. Second, it makes you cry, it's so easy to doomscroll. And, lastly, porn. Unfiltered, underrated porn. The Fitter, my fake Twitter account, is the move. Out of all of the social media platforms, I appreciate Twitter most. I've built a wonderful community, and the education I've gotten because of it is impressive.

A video of a cop terrorizing what appears to be two Black teenagers starts to auto play. I quickly add it to my list of tweets to come back to. Then I scroll past it, because I do not have the capacity to doomscroll now. My mind and energy is for me to protect, and sometimes I have to curate what I allow in. Black murder and the terrorizing of Black people is ever-present, always looming behind every moment here, so sometimes, I need a break from the reminders on social media.

I keep scrolling. Liking funny tweets. I use my Twitter fingers and tweet: *Another audition down. Where's the self-sabotaging ice cream? Also, it's Monday and I don't want to be home...What's the best move.* With the rock-on brown hand emoji.

Within minutes, I have a few likes and responses. I do not look at the responses. I press the on engine button to rev up my 2009 Prius, which I will replace when I make it big. Uncle Justin's offered, saying I don't need to drive anything older than two years. And now, I'm wondering if he's right. The neon orange exclamation point starts flashing, signaling that my tire pressure is low again. A small annoyance. I don't have time or funds to replace the tire, because it'll be my luck that all four need to be replaced.

I start driving northwest from the Arts District in DTLA toward Koreatown. I'm taking the streets the whole way because it's more scenic, and I have nothing to do and all day to do it now that this audition is over and I'm waiting for an answer.

❖

Hours later, after being a tourist in the city I call home, I find myself sitting at the bottom of Zaire's apartment steps in West Hollywood, attempting to shake my self-doubting mood. I should start carrying his apartment key. I have six tacos and two drinks with me. I want to surprise Mr. Surprise himself with food and good company. I'm the good company, obviously. He isn't home from work yet, but I'm sure he'll be pulling up any minute.

I may or may not have had two tequila shots with the

taco stand homie before the spontaneous trip to Zaire's. And, believe it or not, I have a slight buzz. As I wait for Zaire to come home from work and jump with glee when he sees me with tacos, I check Twitter. I'm in a much better spiritual space to engage with the responses I've received from my tweet about the audition earlier.

Many responses are wishing me luck with the audition. It's nice to know complete strangers are really rooting for me. I have a few responses with suggestions about how I could have spent my day. Most I've done before, but there's one I've always wanted to, but have never made time to actually do it.

On Monday nights, at a midsize bar in Hollywood called Da Juice Joint, there's an open mic/jam session. I've seen quick Insta stories about it. Usually I avoid open mics, poetry, and singing, because not everyone is as good as they think they are—like I should be talking. But what I've seen via social media, this open session is the spot to be. I mean, this is L.A., Hollywood, so all of the best background singers, and singers who are trying to break out of the background, jam out at Da Juice Joint.

I like the message that suggests I go to the Da Juice Joint. I screenshot the tweet and text it to Ezra asking if they are down to go. I'd go if they want to go. I won't stay too late. It's Monday, and tomorrow my day starts at six in the morning and it won't end until after six. I might get some Uncle Justin personal time in, too, since he's no longer working during the week.

Ezra texts within minutes saying that they've wanted to go back but haven't had the nerve to go back solo. So, I ask if we are going tonight. To which they respond, what color should they wear? I laugh at the text and tell them I'll pick them up in a couple hours.

I'm getting hungry, but Zaire isn't here. If I eat just one

taco, it'll be okay. I'll have two left. I begin to remove the foil from the plate of pollo asado tacos with extra limes, onions, and cilantro. My mouth starts to salivate. Whose tacos are better than L.A tacos? *Nadie.*

The next door neighbor opens the door and looks down the stairs to where I'm sitting waiting for my man. I wrap up the food.

"Hey, movie star," Alec melodically greets me.

He's an old Russian man. He was an actor back there before he immigrated here, chasing the dream. He's a widower. His wife died last year, right before Christmas. When she passed, Alec didn't come out of the house for two months. Zaire and I would always make food and leave it at his door. The first week he didn't touch any of it. Then the following week, we noticed the containers would make it back to our door, cleaned, and with a thank you Post-it. *Our door.* I mean, Zaire's door.

"Hi, Alec. How's your day?"

He's wearing a white, off-white, a used-to-be-white T-shirt that's definitely older than me. It's tucked into his boxers, which are way past his belly button in the fashion of an older man who prefers comfort over anything.

"The day. Could be better. All days could be better. Vera, you know. She's gone." Alec shrugs and turns his palms inward.

I don't know what to say, so I bring my hand to my heart. I understand.

"I see your famous uncle on the TV on Sunday night," Alec says. "He get fired from the Monday to Friday?"

"No, not fired." I keep it short. It's not my place to give away any details.

"He the only news my Vera and I trust in L.A. That Justin Monroe. I like."

"I will tell my uncle," I say. "He would appreciate hearing that."

"Our son should be walking up any second. Make room for him, please. He's here to help me clean."

Thank goodness he's got help with the cleaning. Since Vera's passing, the stench that comes out of that door when he opens it is ungodly. Zaire and I are clueless to what it could be, so we stay out of it.

I get up from the bottom step because I hear someone walking up the pathway. I assume it's Alec and Vera's son.

And it is. I watch him walk up the stairs and into Alec and Vera's apartment.

"What are you doing here, love?" Zaire sneaks up on me as Alec's apartment door slams.

I jump. I'm startled. We kiss.

"I come bearing gifts. Tacos, horchata, and me!"

We walk up the stairs to his apartment.

As we sit on his plush blue couch, he catches me up on his day and reminds me he and Jordan are scheduled to go to Seattle together this coming weekend. I smile and nod. Internally, I'm cringing. Every time he talks about Jordan, I think about telling him about Jordan and me. But I'm not ready. It doesn't feel right. I also feel slightly guilty for telling him I didn't know what Ezra was talking about when Zaire read my text aloud. I curse Lenay for being drunk and reminding me Jordan and I had sex.

Zaire makes a joke about him and Jordan making sure not to use energy powder while visiting their best friend, Lauro, in Seattle. The Miami reference is embarrassing. Soon as I landed back in L.A. from Miami, I told Zaire all about the energy powder and Rojo's dick. He laughed and called me a lightweight. I really am. Then he said my friends are wild, which is him calling the kettle black, the way I know his friends.

When he finishes, he asks about my audition.

"We don't have to talk about that," I say.

Of course we talk about it. We process my pre- and now post-emotions. Zaire is fascinated by how much I share, the details I include to describe the audition. I tell him I counted each stair to the audition room—eighty-four. I tell him I did the stairs and not the elevator because I wanted my heart beating fast when I performed. The scene I was reading was intense, and that would help my body tap into that energy. I tell him I carried my Mookaite jasper stone in my left back pocket to allow me to be open to new possibilities. It's also a good stone to keep me healthy. And the citrine stone in my right back pocket is to help me interact creatively with the day.

"I don't think I did that great. I sucked. I sucked. I sucked."

He waits for me to say more. I feel myself wanting to cry. He rubs my shoulder, and that makes me drop a tear or seven.

"I just want my big break already," I say, crying. Laughing. Laughing-crying. Crying-laughing "I try so hard."

"Aww, love," Zaire says. "Just keep being out there. It'll come. But even if it doesn't..." Zaire whispers the last part.

I stare at him. Sharply. What the hell, *if it doesn't!*

"I mean, it will," Zaire explains. "But it might take much longer than you want."

Much better.

"Remember you're choosing to do this. Why? Why do you act?"

That's an easy answer. I'm happy he asked it because it dried my tears up. "I act because," I say, and stand up, being kiddish and dramatic, "It. Brings. Me. Joy!"

Zaire meets me on his feet and kisses me.

"Period. Pooh!" he says.

We laugh.

He kisses me more.

"You know what brings me joy?" Zaire asks.

I could guess two things for sure at this exact moment, but I won't. I shake my head no so that he could just tell me, as I mentally prepare to unzip Zaire's pants and make us both feel good.

"You." Zaire looks longingly in my eyes. "You being here. You staying here. That brings me joy."

There it is. Staying here. I was sort of right. Me. Not my head game per se. Me as a whole being, being here, brings him joy.

"Thank you," I say. "You bring me joy, too."

Me being here with him now is so joyous. But I will not say that because I am not ready for the staying here conversation.

CHAPTER TWELVE

Justin: F'd Up

I'd normally talk about this kind of situation with my best friend, Trevor.

But since Trevor is the situation, and he hasn't exactly been talking to me since the night we had sex, I go to the next best thing to a best friend. My nephew, Elijah. I had some dinner and Elijah's favorite Tillamook ice cream delivered. We're sitting in the kitchen/dining table area where it all went down with Trevor and me a few weeks earlier, and I've explained to Elijah how it all went down.

"Whoa, that's kinda f'd up, Uncle J."

"Of course it is," I say.

"And you two haven't talked since then?"

"No."

"For real?"

"Nothing. Except for a few scattered texts that don't say much."

"Can I see?"

I hand over my phone to Elijah and he reads out loud the texts between Trevor and me.

> *Justin: Where you? We gonna talk? Why you sneak out in the middle of the night?*

Trevor: Not now. The note I left says enough. Thanks and sorry.
Justin: That's it?

"Wow, y'all really did it?" Elijah looks up from the phone.
"Yep. Crossed that friend line."
"And how was it? I mean, if that's not too much to ask. I'm kinda curious. Trevor is fine. If he wasn't your best friend and all…"
"It's too much to ask. I'm still your uncle. Some details, you don't need to know."
"Got it," Elijah says. "So, Trevor did a fuckboy move and left? No goodbye or anything?"
"Not a word. Came, snored, and went."
"That really is f'd up, Uncle J. It's not like y'all were some hookups from the apps."
"Exactly. Keep reading."

Justin: That's it? (wide eye emoji) I'm asking again.

"Wow. Two days and no reply. All right. I see you gave him the benefit to reply."
"Something like that."

Trevor: I've been busy. Sorry I haven't responded.

"Everybody's busy," Elijah says and continues reading. "I hope busy is not his excuse for not giving you an explanation. Wait, who am I kidding. You do the same thing, going hours or days without replying to texts sometimes."
"Whatever, Elijah."

Trevor: It is what it is.

I'm back with Sonoma.
You've got that man.
Let's just forget it and let some time pass.
Justin: It's weird to not talk daily. That's all.
Trevor: When you're over your feelings, we can talk.

"Over *your* feelings? That's f'd up. Trevor came to *you.*
Gaslighter."

> *Trevor: And go back to being "best" friends, if you*
> *can handle that.*
> *Trevor: Maybe it's good you're on weekends and I'm*
> *still on weekdays. We need a break.*
> *Justin: Let me remind you. You were drunk and*
> *initiated everything. I never said anything about*
> *feelings. You assumed.*
> *Justin: And now I'm feeling guilty. Because of "that*
> *man" as you say. His name is Jabari, by the way,*
> *if you care to know his name.*
> *Trevor: Jabari. Cute. Like Girlfriends.;-) No need for*
> *feelings. I got Sonoma. You got Jabari. Let's take*
> *a break from texting.*

"Okay," Elijah says. "He's joking. He's not over the
friendship or you."

"That's what I thought at first. But keep reading."

> *Justin: We're neighbors. It's silly we're not even*
> *walking next door to see each other. I'm not*
> *trying to start drama. We just don't need to not*
> *be talking. Not after twentysomething years of*
> *friendship.*
> *Trevor: Gimme some time. Maybe it's me, not you.*

*And don't fuck it up with that man—Jabari—
by telling him what we did. Not gonna happen
again. And you will get over me.*

"Hmm. Gaslighting again. But whatever."

Justin: Were you ever into me?

"And that's where we left off," I say after Elijah hands me
back my phone. "I shouldn't have sent that last text. Haven't
heard from him since."

"That's f'd up." Elijah spoons out a large chunk of vanilla
ice cream from his bowl. "I probably wouldn't have sent that
last text, but what's done is done, and you did it anyway. What
was your intention?"

"I guess I just want…wanted…to know…I don't know."

"It's okay, Uncle J. Stuff happens. I never should have
told you to tell Trevor how you've felt."

"That's the thing," I say. "I didn't. Said he's always known
I've had a thing for him. Without me saying a thing."

"It's f'd up he kinda used you to get over Sonoma. And
now he's back with Sonoma."

"For the third time."

"I can tell you care. And I can tell you have some kinda
feelings still for Trevor."

"Wanna know how I really feel? I feel like a hypocrite.
Talking about my loyalty to Jeanine—and I was completely
loyal—even when I wanted to do something outside our
marriage. And telling you to tell Zaire about you and his
bestie, Jordan."

"Well, I'm not judging you."

"Really?"

"Really."

"Love ya."

"Love ya back."

"So, I will pull an Uncle Justin and ask you 'so what do you think you want to do next?'"

I hate it when people want to pull a "me" on me. "I will move forward with Jabari, and I will not say a thing about Trevor and me. And I will give Trevor space. Eventually, things will all work out, and any feelings that were once there will ease back to normal."

"You believe that?"

"I'll see if I can get on Thea the Therapist's client list," I say. We laugh.

"Good luck with that," Elijah says. "She stays booked. But Zaire got a former boo, now friend, Kenny Kane, who got a connection. Let me see what I can do. You need more friends. I'll see if I can connect you and Kenny."

"Thanks for listening. I value you. And yes, I do need more openly gay or queer friends than you and Trevor. It's hard to make friends in my position, you know."

Elijah tosses out his empty carton of Tillamook, and I finish the last spoon of my ice cream. The front doorbell rings, and then I hear a key fumbling with the lock to open it.

"Who's there?" I yell, heading toward the front door. Wasn't expecting any company, like anyone other than possibly the young ones, who have their own keys. But it's a school night and they wouldn't do a spontaneous, unannounced trip home during the week. Elijah follows.

It's Trevor. Huge smile on his face. Sonoma walks up behind Trevor and spoons him.

"Hey, friend," Trevor says with a singsong tone like Oprah, and makes his way into the foyer. "Oh my God, hey, Elijah. Long time no see."

"Trevor?"

"Trevor?"

"The one and only," Trevor says and widens then focuses his eyes on me. I've seen that don't-say-anything look before.

"We were just talking about you," Elijah says. Shade.

"I bet you were."

"You know it."

Elijah and I look at each other, roll our eyes, and then back at Trevor and Sonoma, who are looking all lovey-dovey once again. Sonoma plants a long deep kiss on the side of Trevor's neck from behind. Trevor looks at me again and smiles.

"Oh. Sonoma, this is Justin's nephew, Elijah. He's a struggling actor. Y'all need to connect."

"Actor. Not struggling. I'm an actor." Elijah and Sonoma fist bump. I fold my arms.

"What are you doing here, Trevor?"

"We have some news to share." Trevor singsongs again. "And we had to let my bestie be the first to know. Sonoma and I have been busy."

Trevor and Sonoma both lift their right hands up. Black bands trimmed in rose gold.

"You're—"

"Engaged!" Trevor interrupts me, then turns around to face Sonoma, who's leaning in for a kiss. "Sonoma and I are engaged."

"Oh, wow." Elijah walks toward the duo. "Can I see the rings?"

"Yeah, for sure," Trevor says. "But how about a 'congratulations' first!"

Elijah and I look at each other. I'm confused. I don't know what he's thinking. But we both go, "Congratulations."

This is all a little much for me.

"Sonoma, Elijah," Trevor says. "Maybe you two can go to

my place. Talk acting. Rings. Something. Elijah might be next, anyway. Zaire, right?"

"Zaire…yes," Elijah says. Then looks at me. "You okay, Uncle J? With me chatting it up next door with Sonoma?"

"Sure, see you in a few." And then I add an untruth that Trevor and Sonoma don't need to know is an untruth. "We still have our dinner reservation in forty-five minutes in Marina Del Rey."

"I'll make it quick," Elijah says and smiles.

Trevor puts a key in Sonoma's hand, and his fiancé and my nephew make their way down the porch stairs and next door to Trevor's place. Trevor shuts the door and walks toward me.

"Hey, friend," he says. "I'm sorry."

"I'm confused."

"I'm sorry for confusing you."

"Well…"

"I'm sorry for coming to you that night and taking advantage of your feelings."

"Thanks."

"That's all?" Trevor asks. "Do you want to yell or cuss or hit me or ask any questions?"

"I want to do all of the above. But let's just focus on questions."

"Shoot."

"You sure?"

"Don't shoot, literally. But you can go. Or I can go."

"I don't know where to begin. But yeah, I have had feelings for you for many, many years. Still do. A bit."

"I know."

"And?"

"I've had them, too."

"And...I mean, we're grown. Does Sonoma know? Whether it's about that night or about any feelings we may have?"

"No. And no. What about that man—I mean, Jabari?"

"No. And no. Do you plan on saying anything, Trevor?"

"No."

"Because? And that's not an accusatory because. I just need to know. For my own sake."

"Sonoma and I have made peace with our differences, our chemistry, our fire. And it feels right. I can't get him out my system. Why complicate it?"

"Gotcha."

"And why complicate it for you and Jabari?" Trevor asks. "It was just one time. It was bound to happen, seeing that we're two men, and we're queer or whatever, and we're besties, and I was drunk, and you're amazing."

"I see."

"Let's not complicate it. I have made peace. I have reached closure."

"Like that?"

"Like that," Trevor says. "I'm good with Sonoma. And I want you to be good with Jabari. And I want us to be good as besties. Don't say anything. I'm not."

"I just don't want it to be weird between us, Trevor. And it might be for a while. At least for me."

"You think?"

"Come on," I say. "Twenty plus years of friendship. My crush on you. We work in the same industry. Confide almost everything in each other. What happens if we do one of our backyard wine nights, get to reminiscing, think about that night, and wonder if there's more where that came from?"

"Then we won't reminisce. Or wonder."

"Trevor, come on."

"Justin."

"Or you and Sonoma get into another fight, and you don't want to be alone for a night."

"Not gonna happen. Sonoma and I are solid."

"Trevor."

"Justin."

"All right then."

"All right then."

"Be happy with Sonoma."

"I will. And you be happy with Jabari."

"Well, there," I say and look around. Nothing to do or hold on to or grab. Awkward. I put a hand out to shake on it. "We'll figure out the next wine down time, then. Friday nights work best for me. Jabari's usually here on Friday nights. You can invite Sonoma. We'll be a nice little foursome."

"A foursome," Trevor says, pulling me in for a hug. "Imagine that."

We laugh and continue our embrace. And I think, maybe, with some time, I'll get used to pretending nothing happened and we'll get back to the normalcy of best friendship.

Or maybe it's f'd up to think we can.

Sunday To-Do List

- 8 a.m.: Alarm 1
- 8:15 a.m.: Call Dad
- 8:30 a.m.: Stretch & Meditate w/gospel & bounce music
- 9 a.m.: Shower
- 9:15 a.m.: Nutrients—cook, have water, vitamins
- 10 a.m.: Plan tutoring materials for Monday & Tuesday
- 11 a.m.: Prepare Monday's spin class routine and music
- 12 p.m.: Bike to Zaire for lunch
- 12:45 p.m.: Zaire Solo Time
- Lunch
- Grocery shop
- Sex
- Meal prep
- 7:15 p.m.: Leave for friends hangout
- 11 p.m.: Rest

CHAPTER THIRTEEN

Elijah: Are We Penguins

The sun is starting to set as we drive west on the 10 freeway. The sky is a magical smoky orange pink, the kind of color exclusive to L.A. because of the pollution. The smog is horrible for our lungs, but it makes for the best sunsets. An unfortunate tradeoff. Traffic is kind this evening, too. Zaire and I are on our way to Jordan's for their biweekly friend gathering.

Zaire and his group of friends rotate hosting friend gatherings every two weeks. After two years of being together, we are doing a better job of incorporating our friends into our relationship. We've passed our honeymoon stage of secluding ourselves from our individual friend circles. Apparently we've had enough of our solo-couple time. Both of our individual circles, mine—Ezra and Lenay—and Zaire's—mainly Jordan, and Zaire's three siblings, Savannah, Langston, and Harlem, or the James Gang, as they refer to themselves—started to complain we were not balancing our time well. And I agree. In our two years together, we've spent nearly every day with each other, but with a few, rare breaks in between due to the busy-ness of schedules.

Quiet as it's kept, it was becoming a bit much for me, so I was happy when our people intervened. So now we are being better at finding the harmony between our individual solo time, our *us* time, our one-on-one time with friends, and the time with our friends collectively. Time management is important apparently in all relationships, not just romantic.

Zaire is driving, per usual. I'm not the biggest fan of driving. I only drive when absolutely necessary. I prefer to walk, rideshare, or bike. It's good exercise and is much better for the environment. We aren't playing any music on our drive. We do this sometimes. We like to use shared car time to talk about random things we see on our drive. We talk about our future and make music together. Zaire is horrible at harmonizing, but that doesn't stop us. I like it. It makes us laugh when there's a crack in his voice or when he's too flat or sharp. And hearing his laugh is one of my small joys. At the moment, the car is silent. I roll the window down just enough to place my hand out to ride the wind. My silver nail polish transports me into thought.

I start humming and whisper singing the tune "He Loves Me" by Jill Scott, and I sound surprisingly damn good. I'm not the best singer, but I can hold a few notes. If I'm singing with an actual singer like Ezra, I sound pretty good. But right now, I sound good. I look at Zaire, smirk, then start singing directly at him.

Zaire harmonizes with Jill—off-key. This is very on brand.

If we didn't have to be at Jordan's, I'd like for us to drive up the coast until we reached Santa Barbara. I'm enjoying this ride. Traffic is light and the outside breeze is so nice. I contemplate asking if we should skip out on the friend hangout just so we can drive. Then I think about all of the bickering Zaire might hear from Jordan because we were a no-show.

I let us return back to simplistic silence. We have a few more miles before we exit the freeway, and I have to prepare to be more extroverted with the cohort of friends.

"When did you know you loved me?" Zaire asks, grabbing a glance at me when he asks.

I am staring out of the passenger window, hypnotized by my nails, when I hear his question.

I am quiet for a moment. I'm trying to find the words. I'm contemplating if I should be honest and tell him the truth. I felt I loved him when I said it during our first Christmas together, during the birth of his nibling. At that point, we'd been dating for a few months. We hadn't had a conversation about exclusivity or monogamy, but we were definitely operating more unified.

"I knew I loved you when I told you," I say. "How long before you told me you loved me, did you actually know?" I return the question with a twist.

"Honestly?" he asks, looking over at me, then back on the road, as he exits the freeway.

"Truth is the best answer."

"Well," he says, taking a breath. "I knew on our first date. I felt a connection with you immediately. Then, when we sang in the Lyft ride on our way to the smorgasbord event, it was like, yeah, I love this dude."

He speeds out all of his words quickly, like he remembers each detail of our first date as if it was yesterday instead of two years ago. I believe him. I gently smile and place my left hand around the back of his neck to massage his head. He likes when I massage his shaved head.

When we find parking and before we get out of the car, I look over at Zaire. For some reason I'm more anxious than usual. Sometimes when I have to be around big groups of people, I get slightly apprehensive.

I know this group is our friends, but I feel uneasy about tonight. It could be that I shouldn't stay out too long on this Sunday night because I have an early start tomorrow. It could be that this is the first time Jordan is hosting since it was brought to my attention I was holding a secret—Jordan's and my secret. I don't like feeling like I'm lying to Zaire.

I should tell him now before we go into Jordan's house.

Zaire looks at me looking at him, and curiously smiles. "What's up, you ready?" he asks, raising his eyebrows up and down a few times.

This isn't the right time to tell him.

"Mantra?" I say.

He smirks. "Mantra."

Then we look at each other square in the eye and recite the chant we made up when we know we are out on the town or at a function and we know we don't want to stay out long.

"Chit and chat. This and that. Drink or eat, then we leave. Don't stay too long, real fun's at home," we say simultaneously.

❖

Jordan's parents own the four-unit Santa Monica apartment complex he resides in. His apartment is a pleasant and easy mile away from the Pacific Ocean. It's a perfect evening to park our car near his home and walk to the beach. Santa Monica is a coastal city bordered on three sides by the city of Los Angeles. Even though it's surrounded by L.A., it doesn't feel like L.A. at all. The vibe here is slower and calmer, but still lively and vibrant. I can see myself calling it home one day, maybe the place I will come to when I retire. Some people retire and move to Florida. I want Santa Monica.

When we enter Jordan's living room, we notice he has updated and upgraded his interior decor.

There's a large elephant ear plant, looks just like the one Zaire has in his living room, even down to the burnt sienna pot it's living in. Two giant portraits of two Black queer-presenting people with painted halos around their heads hang along the wall near the new royal blue sofa. Again, very similar to Zaire's sofa. And Jordan's added two giant portraits, one of James Baldwin and another piece called *Black Is Queen* by the awesome artist Cozcon—again, both of which I gifted Zaire recently. The entire living room and dining area are knock-off versions of Zaire's apartment. For the past eight or so months I've assisted in the transformation of Zaire's flat, so I notice the thievery.

Jordan gives the same greeting he gives Zaire each time he sees him. A loud announcement, "Ayyyy my brother is here," and then he rushes over to Zaire no matter what part of the room he's been in. Then there's the handshake, then the embrace.

He greets me the same way he's greeted me since I've been with Zaire, "Good to see you," with his inside voice. Then there's an embrace. His arms, always wrapping tight. His right hand, always at the bend of my lower back, a centimeter below what could easily be read as inappropriate by others. His six-foot-three-inch body towers over my five-ten body. He always smells like the cologne Black by Kenneth Cole. It's a sweet and fresh musk.

My eyes start to water, as I forgot to take my allergy pill. Between Jordan's nice cologne and the cinnamon-scented candles, my eyes are sure to run a river tonight. Z and I attempt to live a more scent-free life, so I need to take more precautions when Z and I surround ourselves with others.

After Jordan greets us both, Zaire and I split to make our rounds around Jordan's place. I do a quick scan of the room, taking in everyone who's here.

From the looks of it, we're the last to arrive and we might

be the first to leave—my anxiety. I will try not to let it get to me.

Lenay is in the dining area talking to Tasha and Marcus. Tasha is one of Jordan's and Zaire's friends. A beautiful, free-spirited engineer. People gravitate and flock to her. L is definitely a fan of Tasha. I can see them getting together one day, that is, if both of them ever decide to actually be with people for longer than a few weeks. L is still a believer that romantic relationships are overrated and not vital to happiness. Tasha is the president of the my-friends-and-toys-suit me-just-fine club.

Ezra is in the kitchen pouring a drink, looking quite immaculate with their HBO's *Euphoria*-esque eye makeup.

"Finally, y'all here, get a drink so we can start some of these games!" Harlem, Zaire's younger brother, yells on his way in from the back.

Here on this evening are ten of the dozen or so usuals. Mostly Jordan's and Zaire's crew. Lenay, Ezra, and occasionally Jabari are the folks in my no squares circle.

There's usually at least one game that we all collectively play before the night is over. The host is responsible for the game selection. When Zaire and I host these gatherings, our games are trivia word games, because Zaire loves riddles and things. Being a trained actor who still takes classes, I'm used to collective games and improv activities. However, being with Zaire and his group of friends, I've become more accustomed to competitive activities. Tonight, since Jordan is hosting, he's in charge of the group game.

I make my way over to greet Ezra with our special hello: two air kisses near the cheek and a pageant wave. We've done this since we were sixteen. It started off as mockery of when I became homecoming king in high school. I was the girls' favorite stoic thespian, aka their favorite gay. Ezra passes me a tequila drink. Then I head over to get into L's and Tasha's conversation in the dining area.

"What are y'all talking about over here?" I interrupt.

L looks at me with a smirk, knowing I'm intentionally trying to put a damper on the conversation.

"Child, the ghetto," L says. "That's it."

"Precisely, I knew you two wouldn't be talking about much. You do this every time we hang out. All this tongue action and it goes nowhere." I pause and look at Tasha before I finish. "Now *that's* the ghetto," I say and take a sip.

Tasha lets out one loud laugh, then adds, "We were actually really talking about the ghetto. I was telling All-Tongue-No-Action L about this new contract I got in the hood. I'm doing something in the ghetto for once."

Tasha the engineer has clearly had a recent change of heart about working with Black and Brown communities. She doesn't come from "the hood," as she refers to low-income areas, and she only goes to such neighborhoods for more authentic Black and Brown foods.

"Wow, this tongue has a lot of action," Lenay says. I think she's annoyed, maybe insulted. "Thank you very mu—"

"Again, all talk," Tasha cuts L off. "I bet you really do make a good lawyer."

I smile and take that as my cue to exit. My mission has been accomplished—get these two on the sex track. Later, after they eventually have sex without commitment, Lenay will pretend to be annoyed I made it happen. I see it now.

A good twenty minutes go by, and Zaire and I have made our way around the apartment, greeting and chitchatting with folks, then we meet each other in the hall near the bathroom to check in with each other, like couples do when assessing a scene.

"One hour countdown starts now?" I whisper-ask Zaire.

He laughs. "You're really not feeling it, huh?"

"I mean, I'm not *not* feeling it. I just want to have some solo time with you tonight. That's all."

Zaire knows starting tomorrow I'm going to be booked and busy in the coming week. I have spin classes, tutoring, acting class, one commercial gig, and three auditions.

"Solo...solo time?" Zaire asks and licks his sexy lips. "Go ahead, start the countdown."

I grab Zaire's wrist to look at his Apple watch to take a mental note of the time.

"Okay, come on, Negroes and friends. Game time!" Jordan's yelling from the living room to everyone, our cue to get out of the hallway before we get a head start on solo time and start touching each other.

We all gather in the living room, some getting comfortable on the sofa, some using the huge floor cushions—something else Jordan's appropriated from Zaire—as seats, and others bringing in the chairs from the dining table.

"We better not play *Taboo!* We play that too much," Harlem says before Jordan can explain what the game is.

Zaire throws a small pillow at Harlem and tells him to shut up and sit his drunk ass down. Harlem laughs and flops on the sofa next to a cute woman who he's been talking her ear off most of the evening.

Jordan brings over a large bottle of Ciroc with shot glasses and places them in the middle of the living room coffee table. Whatever this game is, I'm becoming even less interested. I've been sipping on my one tequila drink all evening. I'm not drinking anymore, and I'm definitely not mixing alcohols, not this Sunday, not tonight.

I find myself sitting on the arm of the sofa while Zaire is standing up, slightly leaning over my shoulder. I like him leaning on me. His body always feels good on mine.

"Aight, check it." Jordan grabs everyone's attention. "We're going to take it back. Good ol' *Never Have I Ever!*"

Everyone but me has a visceral response. *Never Have I Ever* is all fun and games until it's not. The game is simple and has the potential to be quite hilarious with all of the statements and things people allegedly haven't done. When alcohol is involved, the game turns into being about sex and scandal. The goal is to see who is the most raunchy and the most adventurous, also highlighting who is the most prudish.

Around big groups, when I'm not hosting, I do my rounds and greet people then I go to being a wallflower. I like blending into the background and observing. I think about going to the bathroom to escape the game for a bit. But I don't.

"Okay, so y'all know the actual rules. So, here's the new house rule. If you've done something, you take either a shot or a sip of your drink," Jordan tells us. He talks with his arms and hands, his biceps naturally flexing.

"How many fingers?" Lenay asks Jordan but looks at Tasha.

Tasha smiles, then rolls her eyes.

"Seven fingers. We'll start with seven fingers," Jordan says, raising seven fingers.

Everyone has their seven fingers up and drinks nearby, except me.

"You're not going to play?" Jordan asks.

I shake my head. "I want to watch."

"Boo! What you got to hide?" Lenay chimes in.

Ezra jumps in to save me. "Some of us have couth. And would like to keep it cute. That's why I'm not playing, either."

Ezra and I both flip Lenay off. She laughs.

The first *Never Have I Ever* statement asks those who've ever had sex in public to put a finger down. If I were playing, I'd have to take a shot or two. Zaire as well. But I'm not playing. I'm watching. I look over to see if Zaire has put a finger down, and he has.

Tasha starts the next one. "Never have I ever felt like I had or met a soulmate."

The party's response is all over the place. Some grunt and call it a waste of a statement because it's boring. Others ask to define what a soulmate is. If I were playing, that would be me.

Zaire puts a finger down and takes another shot, meaning he has felt like he's had or met a soulmate. I internally gush. Then I realize I don't know why I'm flattered. He could be talking about someone before me, like his ex-spouse, and I don't know if I believe in soulmates anyway.

I'm not so sure there is only one person for one person. Although life would be a bit easier and a bit less creative if we all knew we really did only have one, the absolute one to look for. If we lived like penguins, we'd know who is and who isn't our soulmate. We wouldn't have to figure out, date, or fuck Tom, Dick, and Harry to find *the one*. We wouldn't have to feel like we had to keep things away from each other. We wouldn't secretly fear cohabitating or turning into strangers down the line.

If we were penguins, we'd know. We'd know who would be our partner, our forever mate. But we aren't damn penguins.

I take another sip of my drink and tune out the next statement because now, I'm thinking.

Maybe soulmates can be a thing, but not as the dominant culture describes. Maybe we have multiple soulmates. Maybe soulmates aren't reciprocal. Maybe Uncle Justin is Trevor's soulmate, and he took too long to figure it out and now they are missed connections.

When I think about deep love, relationships, and someone who makes your soul feel seen and open, I think I've had three soulmates in my lifetime thus far. I'm pretty sure my first soulmate was Ezra. Platonic soulmate. Ezra and I never had a real interest in being romantically involved. During our teenage years, we had sex a few times, but it was more for exploratory reasons. Internet searches and porn weren't like they are now. We are a part of the last generation that still had to figure out things via physical exploration.

My second soulmate was a bit different.

We didn't become boyfriends. We barely dated, if dated is what you would call it. He was an aspiring actor from South Carolina who lived in South L.A. We met in an acting class. A tall, slinky, dark-skinned gentle soul. His southern gullah accent was big and beautiful like his smile. I'm convinced his primary goals for being in the class included softening his native tongue, hardening his standard accent, and being a wrecking ball in my life. He only did okay with the first two goals, but he mastered the third. He deserved an award for that.

He was the first person I took home. I even introduced him to Uncle Justin. When we called it quits, I had to make sure I cleared myself from seeing the world he curated online. I had to focus on me. So, I muted him. He is still muted on all of my social media platforms. In fact, whenever Ezra or Lenay occasionally speak of him with me, we refer to him as the Great Muting. I haven't thought about him in so long. I'm in a totally different emotional and mental space. I'm sure I could unmute him, and I wouldn't bat an eye about it. It's not like we don't cross paths in LaLa land. I see him at some of my auditions. Some, not many. We mostly go for different role types. I'm happy I've done and continue to do spiritual work, because for the most part, in this clear space, I get to really experience and enjoy my time with Zaire.

I look up at my third soulmate. He is cackling about something that was just said, something I half heard because I was off in my own soulmate world. Zaire's laughter pulls me back into the party.

"Never have I ever had sex with two or more people in this room," Jordan shouts and laughs.

Ezra is caught off guard and accidentally spits out their ice from their cup. The drama. I play it cool and look around the room. Some are taking shots and others are laughing. I see Lenay playing cool and looking at me on the low. If I were playing, I'd have to put a finger down, take another shot and ask how does he define sex, because Jordan has definitely had sex with more than two people here. Oral sex counts. But, again, I'm not playing.

I get up from the arm of the sofa and whisper in Zaire's ear. "It's solo time."

Zaire wraps his arms around my waist. "Bet. Let's bounce."

Even if we aren't penguins, we are worth the try at soulmating. I will tell Zaire about Jordan. I *will*.

CHAPTER FOURTEEN

Justin: Wasabi and Hot Tea

We are at the Americana at Brand in Glendale, not too far from the Hills, eating at Katsuya, where Jus and Junior indulge in their favorite sushi rolls with me. I've signed them out of school for shopping and lunch. Just because. The perks of no longer working during the week.

"Is Mom okay?" Jus asks.

"Is someone dead?" Junior asks.

Twins.

"Everything's fine. But we need to talk."

"During the middle of a school day?" Jus asks. "This must be serious. We're glad to be away from campus and all, but still…"

"You good, Dad?" Junior pulls the EarPod out of his left ear, a sign he might actually have concern for me or for what we've got to talk about. And he's got more to say, which means I've got him and his sister worried. "I mean, I didn't need these new Jordans or the denim jacket."

"And I appreciate the Nordstrom spree, Dad," Jus chimes in, "but college is more important than new clothes."

"Well, Thanksgiving is coming up, and I wanted you to have something new to wear for when everyone visits."

"Thanks," my young ones say in unison. "Appreciated."

"But we weren't born yesterday, Dad," Jus says. "Is something up?"

"Dr. Braxton doesn't allow midday off-campus privileges for just anyone," Junior says. I'm surprised he's got more than his usual two-word responses to say today. "Especially to Black students. But whatever."

"I am looking forward to graduation and getting out of the Hills for good," Jus responds. "I appreciate the stellar education, but that place is about as anti-Black as...every place in the U.S. But thank you, Dad. What's up?"

This may be more difficult than expected. But the server comes back to the table and provides a much-needed delay.

"I know you must get this a lot," they go, as they refill our water glasses and check the status of our table, "but my parents used to watch you on TV every night. Could I?"

I turn on the anchorman smile, say, "of course," ask Jus or Junior to decide who's taking the photo of the server and me, and pose with the server.

"Thank you so much, Mr. Monroe," the server says. "This will make my parents' day."

"And give them my regards," I say. "Especially for raising a young one as polite and professional as you are."

That buys a few minutes to decide if this is what I want and should do.

Though I want to talk to them about Jabari, I'm wondering if this is the time, place, and manner to do it. Perhaps I should have invited their cousin Elijah to spend the day with us. Certainly his being friends with Jabari might soften the blow and make it more palatable, especially knowing how much they are disliking their experience at the Hills.

And now I'm wondering if taking them out of school for part of the day, when I know they need to go back and pack soon for the upcoming fall break, is a good idea. What if they run into Jabari? What if they start running their mouths, as teenagers do, to their classmates, and then it becomes a situation for Jabari and the people he works with and answers to? Maybe I should have thought this out a little more.

Jabari assured me he'd excuse them from school for the afternoon and that it would be okay to let Jus and Junior know we're acquainted and that he'd be coming to the house for Thanksgiving dinner. We discussed the pros and cons during his last sleepover at my place, knowing we'd need to give them some advance notice of his visit and our relationship.

"You all are right," I say. "And I'm usually straightforward on many things with you. So, there is some news I want to share."

"Are Mom and Val moving into the guesthouse?" Jus asks.

"Why would you say that?" Certainly, Jeanine would be welcomed back in L.A. and into our twins' lives on a regular basis, but she and I haven't discussed this as part of the co-parenting package.

"Last time we talked to her, she said she missed L.A. and being around us on the daily," Jus says. "But we guessed wrong."

"We moving?" Junior.

"No."

"New job?" Jus.

"No."

"Then what, Dad?" Jus and Junior in unison, again.

"If you'd just listen, I'll tell you."

"Listening." Junior. Pulls out both EarPods, though I can hear the music blasting in them. That's another dad-son conversation we'll have for the thousandth time later.

"All ears." Jus.

I cut to it.

"Your dad's been seeing someone."

"Like a boyfriend or girlfriend?" Jus.

"A boyfriend. Yeah, you could say."

"Like a 'been getting some buss' boyfriend?" Junior pops another piece of sushi in his mouth like he's said nothing inappropriate.

"Brother! Ewww!"

"Sorry, not sorry," Junior says. "About time you been getting some. You straight?"

"I'm good."

"Good. Because getting some is the best thing in the world. So I've heard."

I know he's experienced. But we won't go there now, over sushi. Parental intuition and teenage sloppiness like leaving new and used condoms behind, under, and next to his bed have told me Junior's been active and responsible for a while.

"Well, I'm happy for you," Jus says.

"Thanks," I say. "There's just one thing. And this is why I wanted us to talk in person today."

"There's a thing?" Jus asks. "You're dating. We're happy."

"It's who he is."

"Uncle Trevor?" Junior asks. Then goes, "I mean your bestie, who's like an uncle to us."

"We've seen how you and Trevor are all our lives," Jus says. "I wouldn't be disappointed if you and Uncle Trevor got together."

"No moving houses," Junior says and cracks a smile. "Ha."

I wonder how they've picked up on grown folks vibes between Trevor and me over the years, but I go back to the advice our family therapist often tells me: young ones have feelings, emotions, intuitions, and insights. They're just in smaller and maturing bodies and minds. Too bad they're right and wrong about this one.

"We're not moving," I say. "And your Uncle Trevor and I are still best friends...and *only* best friends."

I will not tell them anything about what's happened between Trevor and me, or how we're navigating the awkwardness. That's definitely grown folks' business for Trevor, Jabari, and me to work through. Maybe Elijah, since he and Jabari are friends, and I don't know how much information sharing Elijah does with my man.

"There's only one other person I can think of," Jus says. "But we didn't want it to be true."

"One hundred." Junior. "Please don't."

"What do you know?" I ask. "Or *think* you know?"

Jus and Junior look at each other, smile, and I know they've either talked about my personal life, picked up on something, or are just being mischievous with each other in the way twins can be without communicating a word.

And since I'm the daddy, I'm not doing them any good playing these reindeer guessing games with them, like I'm the sixteen-year-old. "I've been spending time with Dr. Braxton, the principal at the Hills. He's really nice and he makes me happy. How would you feel if he spent Thanksgiving with us and the family?"

Jus and Junior look at me. Then they look at each other. Then they smile and burst into laughter. I wonder if I've missed an inside joke. Then again, they're twins. Who knows what's going on between the two of them? They compose themselves.

"Fine." Junior.

"It's all right with us." Jus.

"Like that? Really?" I ask.

Not that I need their permission. But I *do* want their blessing. I am trying my best at this single parenthood thing, and I don't want to fail it or my young ones by doing anything that will set our relationship back. Jus and Junior come first. Always. Before any romantic relationship.

"Really," Jus says. "Right, brother?"

"I'm straight."

"You sure?"

"Yep."

"As long as you're sure and you're being honest about how you feel. You two are my everything."

"We know, Dad," Jus says.

"Ugh, feelings." Junior.

Jus grabs my hand. "We've wanted you to find someone since you and Mom split up."

"Can't just be you and your hand forever, Dad," Junior says, cracking a smile. Reaches out to dap and fist bump. We're all holding hands in a weird triangle around the table.

"Too much information there, son," I say as I smile back at my young ones.

"Sorry."

Back to parenting and putting Jus and Junior first.

"So, maybe we can do a meetup, you all, Dr. Braxton, and me before Thanksgiving, so that it's not so awkward in front of the family?"

"That's fine, Dad," Jus says. "We kinda figured we'd be hosting Dr. Braxton over for the holidays. We were just waiting for you to say something."

"What do you mean?"

"Cousin Elijah can't hold water, as you like to say," Junior says. I guess he's all warmed up now that sex has been part of our family talk at lunch. "We know how to mute these headphones when Elijah gets to the good part of his convos with Zaire."

Go figure. "Tell me more."

"Weeks ago, we heard him talking about that Miami trip y'all took," Jus says. "You know Elijah stays on the car phone when he's running us around town on our errands."

"We got on his Insta and TikTok afterward," Junior says, "and started putting things together about him hinting that you spent time with someone in Miami."

"And then last week, he's talking to Aunt Brenda about coming down and what everyone's going to make and that someone named Jabari was coming over and for her to act right."

"And so we get on Google, and Elijah's social media again, and Dr. Braxton's social media, and we kinda figured it out."

"But just wanted to be sure it was our principal, Dr. Jabari Braxton, and not some other random Jabari Braxton. That's a common name in his generation."

"Tell me more." Since they're on a roll.

"Don't get mad at Elijah," Jus says. "He can't help that he talks a lot and we listen a lot."

"So, you've kinda known already, is what you're saying?"

"Yeah." Jus and Junior in unison.

"And do you have feelings about Dr. Braxton and me?"

"Still hate the Hills," Junior says. "And he's wack as a principal."

"But we've got just less than a year left there," Jus says. "And like we decided, Dad, if you're happy, we're happy."

"And anything else?"

"We'll see," Junior says. "But for now, we good."

And with that, I guess I'll trust my young ones that *we good*, as Junior likes to say, and that we'll have a good holiday season together in the coming weeks.

CHAPTER FIFTEEN

Elijah: Table Talk

I can hardly wait for us to park in Uncle Justin's driveway. Zaire is slightly nervous to meet and be with my family for the holiday. And he should be. Though they're generally easygoing and fun to be around, holidays can bring out the unpredictable in everyone.

Our Thanksgiving is collective work. We are assigned dishes. Uncle Justin is responsible for the turkey and macaroni and cheese. The cajun turkey was Grandpa Malcolm's specialty, and now that he is no longer with us in the flesh, the task is left to Uncle Justin. Mom is the dessert queen. She has sweet potato pie and banana pudding duty. Her homemade desserts are painfully exquisite. Gran'Lin is the master of mixed greens: collards, mustards, and sometimes kale. I have yet to taste anyone's greens that can compete with Gran'Lin's—the smoked turkey neck, the seasonings, the simmering, the love in that pot is holy. Aunt Vick, Uncle Ro, and their children deliciously rotate duties on the mandatory Thanksgiving sides: the cornbread dressing—not stuffing, sweet potatoes, deviled eggs, real cranberry sauce, and occasionally a honey-baked ham.

The red beans and rice is my specialty dish. After years of preparing this Louisiana staple, I've perfected my touch.

This year, I'm not going out of my way to order andouille. I'm not even adding turkey sausage. Instead, I am going to add Beyond Meat. I'm sure they won't even notice. But even if they do, I'll tell them it was a new recipe I'm trying out.

"And if you're confused, love," I say to Zaire, "just stay quiet, observe, and join in when you're comfortable and ready."

"Got it, Elijah."

❖

We pull in behind the line of cars.

"Zaire. Gran'Lin is going to love you. Everyone is going to love you," I say, as dry as possible because it's a truth we all know. He's a smooth charmer.

This is our second Thanksgiving together, and last year felt too soon for me to bring him to meet Gran'Lin. He's met the parentals, of course, as they occasionally fly down to L.A. for their favorite Catalina Island visit a couple times a year. I don't know why they like that island. When they fly down, they usually request I go to dinner with them and to bring Zaire. They love Zaire. They find him to be much more stable than some of the others I have introduced to the family.

Before we get out of the car, he holds my hand and tells me, "I believe you, but this feels like another big thing. Like meeting your grandmother and her siblings, and more of your cousins. This is a big thing."

Then it hits me. This dinner is solidifying us as a whole-ass couple-couple. I am Zaire's first real partnership post-divorce. I try not to panic. I try not to panic him. I tell him, "Big things can be easy when you let them be…" I pause and look for the words. "Or when it's meant to be."

He leans in and kisses me, and we head to the door, a

pot of red beans and rice in my hand and a whiskey handle in Zaire's. It's his drink, and he didn't want to show up empty-handed, although Uncle Justin has a whole liquor store in his cellar and the backyard guesthouse.

We are greeted at the door by the twins, Justin Jr. and Justice. Two cameras in our face, they are using two handheld gimbal stabilizers. Fancy. They have recently started documenting things for their new YouTube show: *Just Justice Live!* Teenagers these days. Eye roll. To be young, gifted, Black...and rich.

"You're now on *Just Justice Live!* Before you fully come into the experience, do you give consent to this recording?" Justice says, smiling, making sure she crosses her *t*'s and dots her *i*'s. She's soooo Uncle Justin.

I look at Zaire and laugh. "Sure."

"Awesome! Yes!" they say in unison. Twinning already.

It's nearly 2:30 in the afternoon, which is around the time everyone is expected to be present. We are the last ones to arrive, per usual. I like to be the last one at a family gathering. The goal is for me to make an entrance. Being the family favorite, I get away with being late.

The fresh pine tree scent greets us first as we make our way through the first dining room. The elders must have already gotten the first Christmas tree for Uncle Justin. By Christmas Eve, Uncle J will have three more trees in his house. Nice to have that kind of money and space.

As we get closer to the kitchen, my stomach begins to dance, and memories of all of the past Thanksgivings start to rush through my mind. By the time I turn into the grand kitchen my face is lit up with a smile.

"There he is, my baby boy," my dad says while walking toward me with his arms out.

My dad is a handsome fella. Salt and pepper goatee

mustache. He's pushing sixty and still has a youthful aura. Everyone is in or near the kitchen being a part of the magic that is family. Oh, and what is this, Jabari and his daughter who's in town from D.C. for the holiday blend right in with everyone here.

"Look at my baby!" Gran'Lin looks up from the pot of greens. She's simmering and stirring them because dinner will be served soon. Hers are the only greens the family will eat, even though others have tried to imitate her recipe. Never works.

"My, my, my," Gran'Lin says as she wipes her hands on her apron. "Look at this beau."

She reaches up to hold Zaire's face in the palms of her hands. Zaire blushes. The holding of his face helps to diminish his built-up nervousness. The laying of the hands by elders is a soul balm I am so fortunate to still experience, and now Zaire, too. He doesn't have interaction with many elders these days. His parents and grandparents have gone on to glory.

"Vick, you see how handsome 'Lijah's beau is," Gran'Lin says.

"You know I do. If I was forty years younger…" Aunt Vick says in a joking tone.

"What would you do, Vickie Jean, if you were forty years younger?" Uncle Ro chimes in as he sips his bourbon. I'm sure this is his second glass. He'll have just one more by the end of the night. He'll sip his final glass all night.

"Oh hush, Roosevelt!" Aunt Vick says as she walks over to Uncle Ro. "If I was forty years younger, I'd simply be that, forty years younger!"

Aunt Vick kisses Uncle Ro on his bald head. The elders laugh. My mom walks over to Zaire and me and gives us both a hug.

Zaire and I make our way around greeting everyone.

He meets my older cousins, who are more like my aunts and uncle—they are Aunt Vick and Uncle Ro's children, my mother and Uncle Justin's first cousins. Monica is the eldest of Aunt Vick and Uncle Ro, then there's Deandre, and the youngest, Symone. They all have children ranging from teenage to early twenties, and I'm the oldest of that generation. They are all here, including Deandre's five kids, even though three of the five have different mothers.

There is always that one family member who you greet just out of respect. That person for me is my older cousin-uncle Deandre. He's loud, asks too many questions, and loves to share a good conspiracy theory, even when Uncle J argues him down with facts. Deandre hasn't learned not to argue with a journalist who has a doctoral degree. Love him to pieces, but in a small dose, have to see him once or twice a year kind of way.

Shortly after the greeting, we head to the formal dining room to feast and talk. Since I was a child, one of my favorite things has been to experience the gift of listening to the elders gossip and sharing their stories and lessons about life.

Mom points to the twins' cameras right before Aunt Vick starts the family prayer. "Are y'all gon' put them things down?"

The twins look at each other, then look at her and say in unison, "Um, nope."

Mom looks over to Uncle Justin as if to say *get your bad-ass kids*, but before Uncle Justin can say anything, Gran'Lin cuts in and tells Mom and Uncle Justin *to leave them kids alone*, so Uncle Justin closes his mouth and shrugs his shoulders.

"Go on, Vick, bless the food," Gran'Lin says, winking at the twins. Checkmate.

I squeeze Zaire's hand to signal to him to catch the family dynamics. I gave him the rundown before we got here, and I hope he remembers. I know there's too many names and people for him at once. Gran'Lin and the elders have the final say on everything. It's funny. But I know it's also annoying to Mom and Uncle Justin.

Aunt Vick blesses the food with a prayer that's five minutes past too long, of course. Then we begin to serve ourselves, plating and passing dishes.

There's this subtle moment—if you breathe too loud, you'll miss it, but it's noteworthy. It is right after the last person has made their plate at the very beginning when everyone is eating. When there is just you and the wonderful food. There's a blessed silence that sweeps over, a silence that signals that the love in the food is magnificent. It lasts no longer than a minute, maybe two minutes if you're lucky. Because someone usually notices the stillness and points it out. But when it happens, it's nothing short of love. I love to experience that moment of stillness. Of deliciousness.

"Hey, cuz, I'm surprised you haven't flipped your shit on TV yet, with that fucker in the president's residence," uncle-cousin Deandre yells across the table with food in his mouth. "Pardon my language, Mama and Daddy."

And that's when the silence cloud burst. The stillness is interrupted and likely not to return for the rest of the day.

Uncle Justin responds, trying to sound cute and nonchalant. His whiskey creation hasn't kicked in just yet. Meanwhile, Justice and Junior have decided to prop their cameras up on each side of the table. They are controlling the movements and angles of the camera with their phones. They have not missed a beat with their cameras.

Gran'Lin asks Zaire about his background, his family ties, his work goals, and his future family goals. He says all the things that he shares with me. She approves of his responses. She then asks me about my goals. She wonders why I have yet to be in any big productions. She says I'm way more talented than the actors on her daytime and late night television series. I'm flattered and irked because I haven't an answer that will suffice. I don't know why I haven't landed more roles.

"Gran'Lin, honestly I don't know," I say. "I'm still auditioning, though."

"How long are you giving yourself before you," Mom yells across the table and then pauses, "before you decide to focus on other things like teaching? Or coming back to Sacramento?"

Then the table goes quiet. Everyone knows my mother is jealous that I'm so close to her brother, my Uncle J., and thinks that it's taking too long for me to get my big break. She is hoping I get a traditional job with good health care and a retirement plan.

I look at Mom, and I have no words because I've spoken with her a thousand times. Never have I ever expressed to her that I would stop, that I have any interest in quitting. Me pursuing my passion isn't a fad. Zaire holds my hand underneath the table, and I look away from my mother.

"What your mother is trying to say, son," Dad attempts to add his two cents, trying to be the mediator, "is—"

"What my mother isn't trying to say, but is actually saying, is that she thinks I should stop pursuing my dream and get a nine-to-five job," I say, cutting off my dad. "That's what she's saying."

In the midst of all this, my Uncle Justin has finished his whiskey and pours himself another glass. He doesn't like tension. We aren't even that far into Thanksgiving dinner, and there's tension. And the attention is on me.

"Elijah Golden! Yes, that's what I want for you," Mom says. "I want you to have more stability and happiness. That's all."

"Who says he's not happy now, Brenda?" Gran'Lin asks.

"Thank you!" I blurt, relieved someone is taking my side. Zaire would, but he can't, since he barely knows my family.

What Mother doesn't understand is that outside of all of the bullshit in this weird-ass entertainment industry, I really do enjoy my craft. I get real joy by acting. I enjoy my acting classes. I enjoy the auditions. Whenever I land a gig, it feels like a piece of heaven. A sliver, but a piece, nonetheless. And it motivates me to keep going.

"I have a point to make," I say to Gran'Lin, who originally asked why I haven't been in any major productions yet. "It is not that hot right now for actors like me. Being open about my sexuality, being comfortable with femmeness and femininity. And I'm Black! Ha! And I'm not Billy Porter—no shade. The roles that come my way are a joke most times. The things that get greenlit by straight white men and liberal white women with good hearts don't have me in mind most times. It's trash. But some writers, creatives, and producers are trying to make space for people like me to exist and shine. I'm in this business to be a part of that shift. It's going to happen."

While I'm saying this all to Gran'Lin, I'm kinda saying it to myself, too.

"It's going to come, and I'm going to prove to other little Black, Brown, and queer kids from big-small towns like Sacramento or Fresno or wherever that they don't have to change or bend or fold into what someone else wants for them," I manage to say, while holding back tears. "Okay, I'm done. I'll get off my soap box."

I excuse myself to the bathroom. I need to get myself together.

I want so badly for there to be a day where content creatives show a wide, vast range of life portrayed. I want so badly for the world of media to show the stories I know to be true and rich. I want stories on top of stories about people like my best friend Ezra, a nerd, a drag queen, nonbinary, Black vocalist who can out sing most of the greats—not Whitney, of course—but can't get a break because their being them. I want a story about an Ezra who, I don't know, hates random hook-ups but loves dating multiple people at the same time. Or a story about my other bestie, Lenay, a bisexual, soft stud lawyer, with a white dad and a Black mama, who is probably the funniest person I've ever met and who uses drugs recreationally, drinks too much, but has her life together and doesn't need a romantic partnership to be feel complete. I want a story about queer Brown kids in elementary school who aren't abused, who grow up to be the popular kids, and who become superheroes. There are so many stories I can be a part of sharing. There are so many narratives I want to act in.

I stay in the bathroom for a good five minutes.

I text Ezra and Lenay. *I love you, I hope your thankstaken is full of love.*

As if they were both about to text the group chat, they respond in seconds.

Lenay texts: *Betttchhh get me the fuck out of here! Lol! My dad just punched my Uncle Tony in the face for trying to justify that pig killing another Black person!*

Ezra texts: *I'on know about it being full of love. But there's food for days. I'll send your greetings to cow-town.*

Ezra and I both send gifs to Lenay's texts.

I exit the group chat to see Zaire has texted me a yellow heart. I heart that text and exit the bathroom. I hear table commotion as I walk down the hall. I shouldn't have left Zaire alone with my family for that long. Damnit!

"I don't care what y'all say, I'm not trustin' no white nobody! Not anytime soon!" Uncle Ro shouts at everyone at the table.

"Oh, hush, bae," Aunt Vick says, shooing her hand toward Uncle Ro.

"Things will start to change once we fight them the way they fight us," I hear Uncle Justin say matter-of-factly as I'm making my way back to the dinner table.

"I know that's right!" Uncle Ro agrees with Uncle Justin.

"Let niggas start purchasing guns in high numbers again, and they'll for sure change the laws again," Uncle Justin continues. "That's what they do. That's what they've always done."

His second cup of whiskey is empty. Uncle Ro pours him another glass.

What in the upside down place is going on here? Uncle Justin is being blunt and uncensored. So unlike him.

"Whiteness is a hell of a drug." Uncle Justin is slurring just a hint. "Number one for sixteen years. Ratings slightly down for a quarter or two, and I'm released. Replaced! White people only have loyalty to money, power, and whiteness!"

"My baby!" Gran'Lin yells across the room, above all the other voices and conversations that are being had. "You're being replaced on the *Justin Monroe Show*? How in the hell will they do that?"

"I told you this already," Uncle Justin slurs back. "It's called *More at Four* and *Live at Five*, but whatever. They always find a way to replace one Black for another Black."

Everyone looks lost.

The twins stare at each other mischievously.

Uncle Justin gets up from the table and walks to the backyard. I notice the smell of his Cuban cigar as it wafts into the dining room. He only smokes Cubans on special occasions. And for him, special is like once every five or seven years or so. This doesn't feel special, this evening of Thanksgiving revelations—but whatever this moment is to him, I'm sure that cigar will make him feel better. The twins walk out to Uncle Justin. I get up to peek, just to make sure everything is okay. They hug him, one on each side. Uncle Ro continues to blab inside the house about the plight of Black people and how he wishes he and Aunt Vick could spend his elderly years in the South. But the South is full of the same white people they left fifty years ago.

Next, Gran'Lin gets up from the table and goes to the twins and Uncle Justin outside. One look at Gran'Lin coming close, and Uncle Justin starts to cry. Gran'Lin holds him the best she can, his head towering down to rest on her shoulder, her holding the side of his face with her hand. He weeps. The laying on of the hands is a balm.

Chapter Sixteen

Elijah: We're in Business (Busyness)

Standardized testing is the real villain. Too many so-called leaders in education actually know the harm of standardized tests and yet the tests still exist. Thank goodness the university systems in California are getting rid of—or considering getting rid of—these requirements for college. By now, everyone should know that these tests cannot properly assess knowledge level or measure academic rigor. They are actually gatekeepers, determining which students are worthy. Love standardized tests or hate them, preparing the Hills students to take them helps with expenses. The parents of the Hills students pay me nicely to provide their spoiled teens with tips and tricks on how to get the best score on college entrance exams. But the poor kids and many kids in the hoods don't get special one-on-one tutors specifically for standardized tests. The system is rigged.

Clearly, I am in one of my moods. How I am actually changing the world for the better? Am I doing good overcharging rich families, or am I not doing good because I'm not tutoring poor kids who actually need it? This is the energy I have during this preparation session with my sixteen-year-old student—Caleb Pitt. His peers and parents call him by his *artist* name,

NoMeKi, which ridiculously stands for Non-Melanated King. He is white. He is a rapper/producer/drummer. Like all the others in his white teenage posse at the Hills, they all try to be Black. Try. To me, he is and will only be referred to by his first and last name, Caleb Pitt. Always Caleb Pitt. Never just Caleb or Pitt. It is Caleb Pitt, always. Okay, maybe sometimes we call him Junior's Little Friend, because we think, but don't know for sure, that Caleb Pitt and my cousin Junior might have a little fluid, teenage, angsty friends-with-benefits thing going. Who knows. I dare not ask.

I'm in the kitchen at the Pitts' guesthouse, looking down over the railing to what the Pitts call the Great Room, where Caleb Pitt is supposed to be taking the mock test I prepared. Instead of practicing while I make myself a vegetable fruit smoothie, he is on his phone scrolling. He has one of his EarPods in his ear, and I see him trying to hide the cellular device in his lap. I don't say anything this time because I really don't have it in me to pretend I actually care today. I'm not in the right mood to teach anymore. I'm getting paid regardless, and he neither wants to go to nor needs to get into an Ivy League school anyway. So, these last thirty-five minutes together, I'll let him have this little phone break.

I add green apple, kale, celery, ginger, honey, and lemon to the blender. This will be my pick-me-up snack. A small happy moment. Getting this green juice in my system. I press the blend button and swirl across the marble tiles. Dancing to the music in my head, passing the time. I may just stay up here in the kitchen for at least another twenty-five minutes. Caleb Pitt won't notice and won't care.

"Yo! Elijah, you see this?" Caleb Pitt yells from down below at his desk.

I don't hear him over the blending. I glide my way back to my treat to stop the blender, still dancing to some jazz tune in my head. Feels like Ella Fitzgerald. It's just a feeling, though, because there isn't any music.

"Elijah, you're blowing up! WorldStar!" Caleb Pitt laughs and gets up from the desk.

"What are you talking about, Caleb Pitt? What's WorldStar again?"

"Oh my God, Elijah," Caleb Pitt says and puts his hands up like an L. "Loser."

I'm young, but I'm not a teenager. I have to ask.

I pour myself a healthy glass of smoothie, and I put the remainder in another small cup. I take my first sip, and Caleb Pitt runs up to meet me at the kitchen island. I have a small revelation watching Caleb Pitt run upstairs. Their Great Room is like the size of my apartment times three. Money. I tell you.

"You can have the remainder," I say and scoot the extra glass over to Caleb Pitt.

"My guy, your phone isn't blowing up?" Caleb Pitt says, gulping down the small glass of green juice.

"I turn off my phone when I'm tutoring you. You know, like, how I asked you to do, too."

As if I care about him being on his phone.

"Right," he says in a guilty cadence. "But you might want to check this out, my guy."

He passes me his phone so I can see a tweet of a video.

The video is a clip of me and my Uncle Justin during our private Thanksgiving dinner with our family.

The clip has been edited and shortened to a few minutes.

The clip appears to be a part of a longer video on YouTube.

The YouTube channel is none other than *Just Justice Live!*

The channel of Justin Jr. and Justice Monroe, my uncle's kids.

The video is titled "Black Table Talk: Whiteywood." A play on Hollywood.

The clip has been shared over 10K times, liked 17.5K, and commented 800 times.

I drop Caleb Pitt's phone on the counter. I feel my face flushed. My heart is speeding and my mind racing. I half hear Caleb Pitt rambling on about my family being *too live*. He has no business talking about my family. I tune him out completely.

I come to myself and get my thoughts together. I am downstairs in the foyer collecting my backpack, getting my car keys, and turning my phone on. Today's session is over. I hope I told Caleb Pitt that when I walked out.

I'm in the Prius and my phone has finally decided to activate. As expected, it's over notified: text messages aplenty, a million missed calls, and voicemails galore. I scan my phone to see if any of them are from Uncle Justin. No. As I pull out of the Pitt family's horseshoe-shaped driveway, I call Zaire.

❖

It has been a wild few days. Who knew Jus and Junior's little YouTube show wasn't so little? Their generation are wizards, experts, magicians on all these media platforms. With the video of Uncle J and me becoming one of the twins' most streamed and most interacted-with productions, my life has changed lanes. A few weeks ago, it seemed as though my life was cruising down the far right lane, merging over to a middle lane, taking my time. Coasting. Now, I'm in the far left lane, the speeding lane, with a borrowed Fastrack pass from Zaire, headed somewhere important. Or not.

Apparently, me speaking my truth about the lack of acting opportunities for openly queer actors struck a nerve with many openly LGBTQIA creatives and their allies. Every major LGBTQIA media organization or group either liked, commented, or reposted my thoughts on their social platforms.

I'm sure a lot of the views were because everyone's darling news anchor Justin Monroe was at the table. But if I'm honest, I think I also have a little following. I was looking cute at a fancy dinner table surrounded by my family, who were all dressed and polished. Aesthetically, the video was nice to look at.

I know I was looking cute because I felt cute, and the fans and viewers commented on every detail. For each troll response, and there were quite a few, there were five more positive remarks celebrating my polished nails, my eyeliner, my simple gold chain, my fitted gray turtleneck, and my smile. With the help of the reshares and comments, my following on my social media platforms has increased fivefold. And I've had more hits on my website than ever.

With all of this newfound attention, my phone hasn't been able to catch a damn break. Before the viral, I got an alert every time I had a comment or message on any of my platforms. I rarely set my phone to Do Not Disturb mode. However, post-viral, the notifications are turned off, and DND is the standard operation. If the phone isn't in my hand, and if someone isn't saved under my favorite list, they're not getting through. I have a newfound understanding of celebrities with multiple phones. Where is my assistant when I need one? Calm down, Elijah Golden. You get one viral video and you think you've made it. Ha.

❖

I wake up in my K-Town apartment to Zaire dancing in his briefs. He's singing, "Good morning superstar, good morning superstar!" It's a chilly December morning and he's out of this warm bed, shaking them sexy, thick legs just for little ol' me. He's calling me a superstar because Uncle Justin and I have been making our rounds in the media world. We've been on a few daytime talk shows, one on Logo and another on CBS. We've done three podcast interviews about being Black and queer in Hollywood. Like, I've had my SAG-AFTRA card for years, and now I'm actually feeling like I'm starting to be a part of Hollywood. In a small way.

With these interviews, I've started to learn more about my Uncle J. Like how discretion about his sexuality was a compromise he thought he'd have to make while being a public figure. Or that he has a personal journal called *The Truth Behind the Camera* about his personal thoughts and feelings around the things he's had to report on over the years. He has mentioned maybe turning that journal into a book, similar to the likes of Pearl Cleage in her *Things I Should Have Told My Daughter* memoir.

"Good morning, love." I stretch my arms while getting out of the bed.

"I made breakfast," Zaire says. "Eggs with soyrizo and fresh orange juice."

He leaves the room and heads to the kitchen.

After I do my morning routine of stretching, washing my face, and brushing my teeth, I make it to my small dining table. Zaire is sitting there with his orange juice and empty plate. He doesn't usually wait for me to eat, as he likes his food hot and I take my time to get to the food once it's cooked. I don't mind eating lukewarm meals.

"Thank you for breakfast," I say as I take my second bite. "It tastes delicious. How did you sleep?"

"You're welcome. I slept pretty good. I feel rested and energized this morning. How did you sleep?"

He heads to the sink to wash the breakfast dishes.

"Like a baby. I sleep better next to you. Do you know that?"

"You've told me that before. That's sweet. I sleep well next to you, too."

Zaire winks at me.

The morning is calm and we're home alone. It feels like the right time to have a talk. I'm starting to have a change of heart about living together. Life is too short for me to be worried about things I can't control or things that may not even happen. But before I tell him I think I'm ready to live together, I need to clear the air about Jordan.

"Zaire, I wanna talk to you about something."

I struggle to get this out.

"What's up, love?" Zaire walks back to the table and sits.

I hear my phone ringing in the bedroom. It's the old traditional phone ringtone, which means it's my agent Lyrique.

"Wait, let me get that."

I run to the room to catch the call.

"Hello! Good morning, what's up?" I say as I head back into the kitchen/dining area with my cell.

Lyrique asks where I am at, and I tell her I'm at home. She says good and then starts talking really fast. Then all of a sudden everything fades around me, all except Zaire.

"Shut up!" I scream through the phone, completely surprised.

Life can be so surreal. I look over at Zaire, who is now struggling to put down his orange juice on the table because he isn't looking at where he's placing it. He's looking at me, confused, as if he isn't sure how to translate my expression. The sun is peeping right over his shoulder. It's a blissful moment.

"Okay! Great! Yes! Thank you! Got it. Okay, tomorrow. Yes."

I end the call with Lyrique and walk over to Zaire, who is staring at me.

"I-I got the job," I say slowly, with a tear rolling down my face. "The Netflix show."

"You-you got the Netflix acting job?!"

"Yes," I squeal. "They want me to be the secondary lead character in this new Netflix series!"

Then there are cheers. Then he picks me up and swings me around. When he puts me down, he is still hooraying and dancing. I'm a bit in disbelief.

"Should we celebrate? What would you like to do?"

Zaire runs to the bedroom. I thought he wanted to know what I wanted to do today.

"Zaire! Wait," I yell and laugh.

He comes back with a sweater. He is way more of the turning-up type than I am.

He looks me up and down to see I have not moved. I am still in my pajamas.

"I do want to celebrate, but not right now. I want to go to my uncle's and tell him to his face. You can come with me! Then after, let's fucking celebrate," I say and jump up and down.

"Let's cancel all plans today and go to Six Flags after Uncle Justin or something," I say as I run to my room to get dressed. Zaire loves roller coasters. This will be a fun day.

❖

I walk into the room hoping to be the first actor at the table read. I am not. The writers are here, the director, and the actual star of the series. I remember her from when I used to watch *All My Children* with my Gran'Lin when I was a kid. I didn't know she was still among the living. I may not be the first one here, but I am ready. I've read the entire script thrice since getting it two days ago.

"Well, if it isn't Mr. Hollywood Has No Place For Someone Like Me Elijah…Golden? Is it?"

These are the first words I hear when I reach my place at the table. The gall. She must be a Gemini. I'm not too bothered by her shade. It's been nearly two weeks since the video has gone viral, and I've been receiving mentions and messages ranging from appraisals to slander. Lyrique has been helpful in supporting me through this rapid world spin, surprisingly. Ezra and Lenay have also helped me toughen up by providing me with great clapbacks to the slander. So, this greeting is light.

I pull my chair out from the spot where my name is placed.

"It is I, indeed," I say happily as I sit. "Elijah Golden. I'm happy to be here, and that you know my name. I've known yours for *yeeaaarrsss*. And you've known mine for a week? A newbie I am."

She catches the subtle shade underlining her age.

"Yes, a newbie you are," she says. She gets up from her seat and heads to the nutrition table. She gets some hot water, then turns around and adds, a bit warmer, "Welcome to the team. Elijah G."

I want to tell her it's Elijah Golden, not Elijah G, but instead, I simply say, "Thank you."

CHAPTER SEVENTEEN

Elijah: Confessions, You're a Monster

It's the middle of the night. Zaire is still asleep next to me. I cautiously get out the bed and tap my phone. It's 4:11 a.m. I twisted and turned for the past four and half hours in bed, dozing off for a few minutes then waking up. No real sleep. I got in late from the set and was unable to really wind down. When I got to Zaire's apartment, he was already cozy in bed, dozing off while trying to read a book. He was waiting for me to get here before he went to sleep. He likes going to sleep together.

Tonight is particularly quiet for his block. The crickets right outside the window are making noise I can't seem to tune out. I'm not resting because I'm thinking and feeling. I'm going to write a letter. I ease myself out of Zaire's king bed and tiptoe out of the room. I sit at his living room office station. I take a sheet of paper from his printer and see where this morning's heart takes me.

> *Zaire, Love, Zad,*
> *This is a first, writing a letter to you. Sorry ahead of time if this is all over the place. I'm sleep deprived.*
> *As I write this letter at your desk in your living room, you're asleep in your bed. Your apartment is*

so peaceful right now, even in the middle of gay L.A. I have the same feeling here as I do at my own home. I feel calm. Lately, though, I have not felt calm. I've felt confined with my own thoughts and trapped in my past. I'm writing you this letter now at four in the morning because I couldn't sleep, and there are things I have to get out so I can move forward. So we can move forward.

I'm still getting used to this new routine of life on the set and love life. I am doing what I love to do, and I'm getting paid more than I've ever been paid before. Those things are great. Then there's you, there's me, and there's us. This past year, I've struggled to figure out the separation between us—where you begin and where I end. We've felt so tethered. It frightened me. It frightens me still sometimes. I've never allowed myself to be so intertwined with another person.

What I am learning is, love can be easy. When it has not been easy, I've been the one getting in the way. I've dodged really talking to you about moving in with each other. I've dodged and prolonged it because I was scared as hell. This morning while everyone is asleep and only God is listening, I want you to know, I am still scared, but not of you or us. I am scared of what could happen. I am scared of losing this easy love. But I'd rather do it while being scared than not try at all. That is more my brand anyway. Doing things scared and making the best out of it. Which leads me to the next thing.

This may be a hiccup in our easy love, but I have to let it out because I can't go one more day not sharing things with you. There isn't a sweet way to say this, so here is the thing that I've been holding.

I've been intimate with Jordan, twice. Both times before I knew you. I never told you because once I realized that was information you should know, we were already months into nurturing this easy love. And I simply didn't think it was something I should share. I can see now that was not the right move.

When you read this, I'll be at home. Allowing you space just in case you need it. I'll be open to receive whatever comes next. Scared and all.

I hope you know I love you, and I am sorry for withholding.

TLDR: Your bestie was in my rotation, and I didn't tell you. But I need you to know because I'm ready for us to move in with each other. If this is still an option, I am here. If it is not, I am still here.

Love,

Elijah Golden, aka your superstar

I place the letter on his dresser with his keys, wallet, and Apple watch. From the door frame I take a look at him, his arm covering the spot where my body would be. I want to walk back and kiss his forehead, but that might wake him up, so I blow a kiss in the air.

When I leave and start walking down the stairs to my car, I feel the tears of quiet guilt and the fear of loss. I pull out of my parking spot thinking I'm headed home. Instead I drive to Uncle J's.

❖

Hours later, Uncle Justin is washing our lunch dishes and asks if Zaire has texted or called. He has not. Of course, that's been behind every thought and action today. After I arrived at

Uncle Justin's in the wee hours of the morning, I slept in my honorary bedroom.

I texted Uncle Justin on my way to let him know I wrote a letter to Zaire confessing, and that I would let myself into his house and sleep in my room. I knew he'd be asleep and would read the text when he woke up.

I don't have to be on set until tomorrow afternoon, so being here with Uncle Justin is what I will do to distract myself. But Uncle Justin isn't really distracting me. He's busy asking questions about Zaire.

When do you think he'll respond? Your guess is as good as mine.

Does he usually respond to you right away? Unless he's busy. But even then, he usually tells me he'll respond when he's free.

What do you think Zaire is doing now? At the office working. Or maybe having lunch right now. I don't know.

Why is he asking me all of these questions? Did I come here to torture myself? I probably did. The damn subconscious.

I excuse myself from *Justin Monroe Kitchen Talk* and go to the gym room in the guesthouse out back. Uncle Justin recently ordered a new curved treadmill I've wanted to try since it was delivered. I figure a little cardio run with music blasting may get my mind clear as I wait for Zaire. I go into the gym room closet to get some running shorts and a T-shirt. It looks like a department store, and I love that I can pick out clean gym clothes anytime I want at Uncle J's.

I run a good three miles. As the sweat drips down my chin and onto the treadmill, I start to ponder what I'm doing here at my Uncle Justin's. Running? Where am I going? Nowhere.

I stop running.

"Hey Google, stop music!" Why in the hell hasn't Zaire reached out to me yet? I know he's read the letter. He's had to.

I'm dripping wet on my way to the bathroom to shower, and I FaceTime my go-to's, Ezra and Lenay.

"Mm-hmm," Lenay says as she appears on the screen. She's in her office.

"What happened?" Ezra says, driving somewhere in their car.

I take a deep breath. "I did it. I told Zaire."

"Told him what?" they both ask.

I tell them all about my four a.m. spiritual experience that made me write Zaire a letter. Aaliyah style. Handwritten. Four pages.

"A letter?" Lenay drags. "All right, Gran'Lin."

"Well," Ezra pauses, then adds, "I like it. Good for you, friend."

"I guess. So, what did he say?" Lenay asks as she gets up from her desk heading to close her office door.

I tell them that he hasn't said a word. I haven't heard a word from him. I share that this isn't like him to simply not respond to me. They don't like this. They tell me to call Zaire.

"Not avoidant!" Ezra yells. "I know he's not avoidant, not in his thirties."

"Right!" Lenay agrees.

I do not feel it's my place to call, but they bombard me with questions that get me riled up again. He's had all day to think about my letter. He could have at least texted me that he's read it and that he needs time to be by himself. Or something. They both agree with me.

"So, what are you doing to do?" Lenay says. "Is he home? If he is, go over and talk to him."

I turn off the shower I must have turned on at some point in this conversation. I open Zaire's contact on my phone to check his location. He is headed toward his apartment from what looks like his office.

"You're right. I'm worth a response." I walk from the bathroom to the bedroom to get my keys. "I'm going to go over to his apartment."

"Oh, chile, let me know if you need me. I'm on standby," Ezra says, exiting FaceTime.

And like that, I'm in my car driving down La Cienega Boulevard. When I get closer to Melrose, I check his location again to see if he's home. He is not. He's at Trader Joe's. I've had Jazmine Sullivan playing the whole drive, so I'm not entirely sure if I want to wait for him at his apartment. Trader Joe's, here I come.

I'm walking fast up the stairs from the parking structure. I told him I love him, I'm ready to move in, and he hasn't responded, all because I had sex with his friend before I knew him. That's ridiculous. We are going to get to the bottom of this shit, right here in this Trader Joe's on the corner of Poinsettia and Santa Monica Boulevard in WeHo. Jazmine Sullivan wailing in my EarPods got me all emotional. I don't want to lose Zaire.

When I enter the store, I slow my pace because I'm out of breath and I don't want to look a mess speeding throughout the store.

I search the small produce area and find Zaire near the register in the wine aisle. I stop walking and I breathe. I take out my EarPods and catch my breath. Then I walk up behind him. I tap his shoulder.

"Hey," I say slow and soft. I definitely should have rehearsed something on the drive over.

"Hey! You spying on me?"

I wouldn't call it spying per se. But, sure. I don't answer the question because I'm asking the questions.

"Why haven't you responded?" I say. "Did you read my letter?"

"What are you talking about?" Zaire looks confused. "I *did* respond."

I go to my phone and open my text messages. The last text I got from Zaire was from yesterday afternoon asking me if he should get an Instant Pot, to which I liked the question, meaning he should get the damn Instant Pot. I place the phone in his face to show him my phone and the text. Nothing new from Zaire.

Zaire takes my phone, exits out of the text messages. He uses his pinky finger to swipe the screen. He opens my email. He puts the phone to my face so I can see I have an email from him from 7:42 in the damn morning.

"Your notifications are still off, I see. Let me pay for these things, I'll meet you outside. Read that email."

Zaire side-eyes me.

I take my phone and collect my ego and I walk outside, sit on the nearby public art bench, and open the email.

Elijah Golden,

Well, since you're taking it old school, I'll do the same and email. Good morning. I hope you're sleeping better. I wish you could have spoken to me earlier about what you've been holding on to. Seems like it has caused you a lot of unnecessary stress. Yikes. I knew about you and Jordan. Before you met him, I showed him a picture of us on our first date. He told me y'all had sex before. It slightly bothered me for a good four minutes. The ego. But then I moved forward. It makes no sense to feel weird about that. It was before you and I. And from what he shared, and now you, it really was just sex. We can talk about this more if we need to, I'm open.

What is thrilling to know this morning is your

desire to give our cohabitation journey a try. What a treat. As you know, I've lived with a partner before, but what you may not know is that you are the first person/partner that I've actually wanted** to live with. I'm open to talking about this, too.

If you would like to have dinner with me, maybe we can talk about these things and dream out loud. Let's dream about the places we'll live, the places we'll travel together. Having a future with you is the real treat.

TLDR: I know about you and Jordan. Heauxs. We're good. Dinner, my spot?

Love,
Zaire aka Zaddy

After I read the email, I mark it as a favorite. That is when I notice Zaire is standing right in front of me.

"You're a monster!" I yell, looking up at Zaire.

Zaire laughs and asks me what I mean. I say he's known all of this time and has never brought it up to me.

"Same could be said about you!" Zaire laughs.

"Touché," I say, and we hug. I squeeze him tight.

When we get to the parking structure, Zaire walks me to my car. I kiss him. I haven't kissed him in what feels like too long, although it was just yesterday.

"So," Zaire says, looking me in the eyes, "when are we moving?"

Lord. This guy.

PROJECT LIST

- Jabari, Justin and Justice…and Jeanine?—personal and all
- Genetic health issues—personal, Jabari
- Netflix; Black shows; Diversity; possible story?—Darnell; sources
- Black representation in media, tv news, history; potential story—personal
- Keep Ojai; for now—Felicia
- Relax—personal
- Deplorables, anti-Blackness, D.C. politics, Hillary warned us & nobody listened; potential story—personal, sources
- Is there a future, career potential in rap music?—personal, Elijah
- Do Justin and Justice need security at college?—personal, college campuses
- Kamala, Stacey, Keisha, Maxine, and believe Black women; potential story—personal
- Update my will; update parents' wills; does Jabari have his finances situated?—personal; Elijah
- What would I do if I wasn't a journalist and a parent?—personal
- Having kids after your kids are grown; potential story and personal—personal
- Stop delaying vacation
- Where do people vacation in these times?—personal; contacts
- What would life be like as a regular person? Without caring about job, status, appearance, or people knowing me?—personal, Iyanla, Thea the Therapist
- Love in the forties, fifties, sixties, and beyond; Black love; potential story—personal; contacts

CHAPTER EIGHTEEN

Justin: No New Contract

"...and cut!"

I am co-anchoring the five o'clock newscast on a rare weekday today with Ke'Von Carrington. His new co-anchor is out on maternity leave for a few weeks, so while she's out, the station has asked me to join Ke'Von as part of a rotating guest co-hosts stunt to boost Ke'Von's ratings. Since my departure from weekdays six months ago, Trevor has soared to number one, and I couldn't be happier for my best friend. Not that I'm secretly wishing for Ke'Von Carrington's demise. I do support Black success and excellence. When it's excellent.

This four-minute break for commercials will give me time to check for any text messages from my young ones, who are spending spring break with their mom in Maine, and from Jabari, who's spending his spring break at my house in Ladera Heights. I love that man.

And I love Jabari enough to mask up as the director of today's newscast comes storming his bony dirty-khakis-wearing butt over to my side of the anchor desk. I've overheard Ke'Von make snide remarks to the makeup person and whoever he talks to on his cell during commercials about my masks, hand sanitizers, shields, and precautions. This new virus we've been reporting on is turning into a pandemic, and I'm hoping it's a few days before station management decides we can do newscasts safely from our own homes. The technology is there, and the station has the cash to make remote work happen. They just need to make it happen, as Mariah belts out every morning on my speakers as I get my day started.

"Justin!" I hear bony-butt, the one who's not even thirty, yell my name as he speed walks onto the set. "Who told you to improvise and take 'Chinese virus' out the script that I wrote?"

"I did. I'm not saying that racist shit on the air. I don't care who wrote it."

"When I write something for you, you read it," bony-butt news director yells and slams his hand on the desk. "You got that?"

Ke'Von, my co-anchor, maskless and getting his makeup re-applied during break, turns my way. "Why does everything have to be about race with you?"

I roll my eyes as Ke'Von, who's Black and who should know better than to say some whitewashed bullshit like that to me.

I whisper to him, "Don't do this race stuff with me in front of mixed company. We can discuss when this newscast is done."

"We can do it now," Ke'Von says. "We've got three minutes before we're back on air."

"Say what's on your mind, Monroe," bony-butt news director says.

"I mean, it's not like half the world doesn't know what you really think about race and white people," Ke'Von says. "With you and your little hoodrat kids and your Black family going viral with all your divisiveness."

True. My young ones have introduced me to a whole new media world I wasn't aware of. I have followers. Hits. Reposts. A new generation of young activists, scholars, and community leaders who affirm what I thought was a private family moment as their reality. As the reality of young people working for social change in the U.S.

On the other hand, while *Just Justice Live!* has given me a new boost of fans and followers, it has been a challenge, in an interesting way, for Jabari.

Immediately after the family Thanksgiving footage aired, Jus and Junior started a series of *#BlackAtTheHills* videos. These, too, went viral and connected other Black students at elite, private high schools about the bias, microaggressions, and exclusion they experience at these campuses. The videos didn't sit well with Jabari at first because they put him, and us, in a precarious situation.

But Jabari saw their truth. He realized he was not giving the Black students at the Hills the culturally responsive education they wanted and needed, and explained this to his advisory board members. But when the advisory board tried to force his hand and permanently suspend Jus and Junior, Jabari came clean about his relationship with me and his role in my young ones' lives outside of the school, and did not recommend their suspension. He resigned instead. Took an Assistant Principal position at the Melina Abdullah Academy of Pan-African Consciousness in Baldwin Hills. And my young ones followed suit, left the Hills, and are finishing their final months of high school at the school where Jabari works.

I am proud of Jabari and my young ones. They are brilliant. Hoodrats they are not.

"Hoodrats?" I say, my protective father role emerging front and center in the two minutes left before we go back on the air. "Fuck you, Ke'Von. Don't think I forgot about your East St. Louis upbringing when I took you in as my intern and mentee. Bad teeth. Cheap wardrobe. And everything you told me about your dad not being around, your twelve half-

and step-siblings, multiple moves…forget it. I won't go there, because that's not your fault. And nothing's wrong with East St. Louis."

"Go there, old man."

"Don't you ever talk to me about being a hoodrat, Ke'Von. And don't you ever bring my young ones into a work conversation. Keep their names out of your mouth."

"It's already a work conversation," Ke'Von says. "We have been tiptoeing around you trying to avoid setting you off, fearing you'll call everything racist around here at the station."

"Because most of what's happening in the world right now *is* racist. And I'm not going to be the talking piece for that propaganda coming from those grifters in the red hats."

"Whatever. I can't wait till this week working with you is over."

"It's going back in, and you're going to say it like it's written," bony-butt news director yells. "Understood?"

"Don't talk to me like I'm your child." I point to Ke'Von, then to bony-butt. "I'm a grown Black man, and I've been on the air since both of you were in diapers."

"It's apparent," Ke'Von says. "The way you've let your hair go gray since you're no longer lead anchor."

Low blow. But true. Weekends are more laid back than being on the Monday through Friday shows. But whatever. I've gone a little gray—salt and pepper, the elders would say. I've put on a few pounds. I stopped getting the occasional procedure to touch up my facial lines and refresh my complexion.

"Fuck you," I say to Ke'Von. "I mentored you through that NABJ program when no one else would give you time of day."

"Whatever, boomer." I don't respond. My young ones use that same line when they're frustrated with me. Not a big deal.

"And fuck you, too," I say to the news director. "I'm not spouting some racist bullshit you got from your mama."

"These. Are. Facts. Do. Your. Job." Bony-butt is raising his voice. At me.

"Don't talk to me like that." Surprisingly, I'm keeping my calm, not buying into the energy Ke'Von and the news director are throwing my way. "And by the way, where's your mask? I've already said to you and everyone else around here, don't talk to me without a mask on."

"There's nothing scientific about masks. Do your damn job, boy."

"What did you say?" I ask.

Even Ke'Von stops the makeup person from touching up his face to lean forward.

"Nothing."

"You said something."

"Niggers are all the same," bony-butt news director whispers, or thinks he's whispering, just before he backs away off the set. "And we're back on in five...four...three...and Justin, banter, and introduce the sports segment."

The sports anchor, Yari Roman, walks on set and to her standalone desk spaced away from where Ke'Von and I do the news. We're supposed to make small talk and then transition to let Yari tell L.A. the latest on the Dodgers, Lakers, Sparks, Clippers, Galaxy, and all the college and high school teams in the L.A. area. But I don't feel like making small talk.

"I just got called a nigger by the person directing today's show," I say to the viewers and not to Ke'Von and Yari. "I can't do business as usual now."

Ke'Von and Yari are silent as I stare at the camera. I don't know what to say. Actually, I do.

"So, here are the facts. The director of this newscast called me a nigger. And wants me to share lies and fake news with you all, our viewers," I say.

"Cut to commercial," bony-butt yells.

"No commercial, I'm talking," I say and continue. "I am off script now. But I need to speak to you—my faithful viewers—who've stuck with me through marriage, divorce, being a single father, coming to terms with sharing my sexuality, and seen me go gray and gain a few pounds since I got moved to weekends. I love and respect you too much to lie to you. I just got called a nigger by our news director right before we came back on the air—he ain't think I heard him, but I did. We all did. He demanded that I call the coronavirus the Chinese virus. I will not do the racist and xenophobic work of the people who never should have won the election in November 2016. That's a whole 'nother story. My contract here at the station will be up shortly after the November election in eight months or so, but I will not be staying here until then. This is my final newscast. I love you, L.A. I'll see you soon, unless this segment goes viral and I don't work again in this industry."

I take off the lavalier microphone pinned to my suit jacket.

Put on my mask.

Push back from the anchor desk.

Get up.

And walk off the set.

Live at five.

CHAPTER NINETEEN

Elijah: S.I.P.

I hate feeling unwell. I am a firm believer that you are what you eat, think, and speak. That's why I try to keep in mind what I consume in all areas of my life. Sickness is inevitable for many of us, as some things are genetic. Some sicknesses you simply can't control. I try to concern myself with health things that are systemic and are in my control. Food, water, movement, meditation, and the sun are my medicines. So, when I get sick, which is rare, I'm thrown off, then I'm grateful because my immune system fights off colds and flu literally in a day or two. But this time I can't seem to shake whatever it is that's going on with me.

"Good morning, Mr. Golden, I'm Dr. Pherribo," the doctor says as she enters the room, wearing gloves and a face mask that covers her mouth and nose. This is unusual attire, but maybe this is standard protocol in the Hollywood medical world.

"When did you notice you had a dry cough or when you couldn't taste your food?" she asks as she looks over the notes in her electronic tablet.

I look over past her shoulder. There's a long pause. I place my finger on my temple right before I start to rub my head, hoping to remember. Dr. Pherribo assures me an estimate is fine. I want to tell her, but I can't remember. I want to tell her that my life has been so busy with being busy that sometimes it's hard to slow down. That's why I'm unsure when the coughing started. I refuse to share that, so I tell her the tasteless food a few days, the cough over a week. "I think it's a bad flu."

"That's a possibility," she says as she places the tablet down on the counter and heads to the glass cabinet to retrieve a syringe. "We are still getting more information about this, but…" She pauses, facing me with her back at the cabinet. "I think you may have something a bit different from the seasonal flu."

Dr. Pherribo walks a little closer to me and places the syringe on a small metal tray. She then takes out a long Q-tip.

"I will have to take blood. And I will use this cotton swab applicator to wipe the inside of your nose, going up each nostril."

I'm fine with the needle, take my blood, that's cool. The Q-tip up my nose, however, that's intrusive. And I have never heard of this before.

"Will it hurt? Going up my nose?"

"It may be uncomfortable. I'll be gentle."

She takes my blood. Then she asks me to lean my head back just enough so she can insert the cotton swab. I follow the instructions.

It feels weird.

Feels too far in.

I want to grab her hand and push her away from my face.

I squeeze the armrest of the chair I'm sitting on.

Then she takes it out of my nostril and tells me to brace again for the other nostril.

This time my eyes water and a tear rolls down my face. It isn't that painful, it's irritating something, that's why the tears are coming.

"Okay, that's it," Dr. Pherribo says and places the Q-tip into a small container.

I want to tell her to do whatever she has to do. Give me a pill, give me a shot, a syrup, whatever, because I don't like to feel off, and I need to feel better at work.

"Whatever this is, do you think my cough is contagious? I still need to be on set tomorrow."

"Actually, Mr. Golden," she says, "the entire set may have to be paused. Let me explain to you what we now know about the virus you may have."

CHAPTER TWENTY

Elijah: Beyoncé

Dear diary,

You know when Beyoncé told the world to stop, then to carry on? That's this. We are all in the world-stopping phase. Most folks I know are working from home. Non-essential activities are closed. Hospitals are overcrowded. Restaurants are struggling. Gyms are closed. All Hollywood TV and film productions and NYC theatre productions are shut down. All my performer friends are out of work. The streets are eerie. Zoom stock is flying through the roof. With virtual work, exercise, and happy hours, we are all Zoom'd the fuck out. The world is what Ezra calls the ghetto.

I am functioning with unemployment, family funds aka Uncle Justin and the parentals, and the little savings I have from my first major gig. Don't be surprised if I open up an OnlyFans to get cash flowing.

Never mind. My family would flip.

I know I will find my peace in this moment in

time. I know I will adjust to this new normal. But today is not that day.

Today, what I know for sure is that I am looking forward to the day we are in the clear from this virus and life can carry on.

CHAPTER TWENTY-ONE

Justin: Easy Love

I can't believe I'm getting married today.

And having a real live wedding, complete with a full party, live band, catered soul food dinner, and all the friends, acquaintances, and family I can fit in my backyard and part of Trevor's adjacent backyard. The party is that huge. I'm feeling good and ready. And I promise myself to stay in the moment. Not get worked up about details. Not think ahead to our honeymoon trip to New Orleans—the Big Easy—in a few days.

From the time he moved in at the start of the pandemic to us finally emerging from it, Jabari has been a dream partner.

I knew he was a keeper even as early as the Miami trip. But after he accepted what had happened between Trevor and me without any hesitation, doubt, or guilt-tripping on his part, it confirmed he was the one. The only one. Sealed the deal, so to speak. I knew I had to say yes when he asked if I'd be willing to give marriage a try a second time around, to be his husband.

The theme we've chosen for today is "Easy Love." It fits and makes sense. Surviving a pandemic makes you want to make things easy.

The wedding-planning process. Easy.

The process of getting to know each other. Easy.

Living with each other during a pandemic. Easy.

During the shelter-in-place days, I learned to slow down and allow things to be easy. Even when easy wasn't my mode of operation. With Jabari by my side and months of sitting at home, I started to hone in on what brought me joy. The silver lining of pandemic—reflection time.

And that reflection time turned into journal time. And journal time turned into writing down stories. And writing down stories turned into a memoir. Mine.

Starting with finding real love in my forties. Who'd have thought that?

Who also would have thought I'd walk away from a multi-figure job and career that once brought me joy? A career that only reinforced a public persona, other people's perceptions, and perfectionism. Just so that I could be liked by my viewers, my fans, my journalism colleagues, and all the family members I would often brag about floating. As if keeping everyone's bills paid was a badge of honor to throw in every Monroe family member's face at family gatherings.

And though being number one at everything I put my mind to has brought many great material things for this small-town Black boy from Sacramento, like this home where we are hosting our love ceremony today, the Ojai home, overpriced high school and college tuition, more clothes and gadgets than my young ones need, having enough to live on without having to work again if I don't want to, the pandemic gave me the opportunity to ask one question—what really matters, Justin?

Does being the first, the perfectionist, and the busy give me joy? Do material things? Does having no time for myself? Does keeping a schedule that's packed, booked, and busy?

Does having family and a bunch of strangers running your young ones around town? I think not. The pandemic, plus adding some sessions with Thea the Therapist, gave me time and opportunity to reflect. Learn to chill. Revel in joy.

Knowing the twins are doing well mentally and spiritually in D.C. at Howard University, their dream HBCU campus brings me joy. Seeing my nephew, Elijah, survive his own touch-and-go moments with the virus and emerge from it alive brings me joy and thanks. Watching him ascend to become *the* Elijah Golden with steady work and the high-quality roles he wants as an out, queer Black actor who's happily loving Zaire and Zaire happily loving Elijah brings me joy. Seeing Brenda come around and have pride in Elijah's blossoming career. Joy.

Teaching one course a semester on the History of Black Journalism at a local community college brings me joy. Leading free Writing Your Life Story and Black Futures evening classes at the Melina Abdullah Academy for Pan-African Consciousness for people who never get a chance to set foot on college campuses brings me joy. Doing the *Just Justice Live!* show with my young ones, when they want me online with them, is a joy—and I'm convinced Jus will follow in my footsteps as a journalist, while Junior may make his mark as a songwriter, composer, musician, and, dare I say, rapper.

Being a source of inspiration for others brings me joy. Enjoying Trevor's friendship, watching him reign as L.A.'s number one anchor, and still meeting his ongoing parade of dates and app appointments after yet another Sonoma breakup—I hope he gets his happy, one day—is still a joy. Sharing simple, fun, sexy days and nights with Jabari at our place in Ladera Heights brings me joy. Having both our families here to celebrate us is a treat. Having this late summer wedding on Jabari's fortieth birthday brings joy to both of us, plus his daughter and family, my young ones and family, and my former wife, Jeanine, who's walking me down the aisle today, while Elijah's friend Ezra sings an original song they composed for today—"Easy Love."

There are experts who get real joy at wedding planning, catering, doing music, setting ambience, getting everyone from their home locations to L.A. and settled into their respective hotels. I let them do it.

After Jabari and I both speak our vows and all the other formalities that go with a love ceremony, I'm happy we are nearing the end of this part of the day. I'm ready to eat, dance, and get down!

"Speak now or forever hold your peace," Lenay says.

She looks at Jabari and me.

She looks around at the audience.

I smile at Jabari, who's holding my hand as tenderly as he did the first time I invited him over for a backyard date at my place. He still gives me shivers when he touches me, looks at me, smiles at me. His oh-so-masculine-scent, the signature scent he wore on our first date here, still makes me go fuckfuckfuckfuck in my head. And his yellow tie looks so good on him, complementing our matching summer gray suits. The yellow accents adorning the backyard, the golden tent covering the dance floor, seeing the various shades of yellow on Black and Brown skin of our guests, the golden hour lighting making all of us look so beautiful. Joy. And that we're all vaccinated and able to be close together again. Unspeakable, life-affirming joy.

"Anyone?" Lenay jokes. "It is both their second time around in this marriage thing, after all."

Laughs from the audience.

"Okay, well, let's continue," Lenay says. "We all know

the first time for both of them was for show. No shade to the exes. And this time, in their forties, is for love."

Jabari and I are still holding hands. Staring at each other. Smiling at each other.

"Black sho' don't crack," Lenay says. "Okay. Back to the ceremony. Seeing no objections."

"Wait!" Trevor says, jumping up from the first row.

We look at him. I hear gasps from the audience. I am a bit surprised. He and I put that part of our story to rest. What could he possibly be doing?

"Die!" Gran'Lin jumps up and shouts, "Just die!"

At this moment I know this is all a joke. Trevor and my mother have decided to remake the infamous wedding scene from the popular eighties and nineties show *A Different World*. The scene with Whitley, Byron, Dwayne, and the late great Ms. Diahann Carroll as Whitley's mom. I get it now. An inside joke.

"Just kidding," Mom and Trevor say, and burst into laughter.

The drama.

I break from the ceremony formalities, laugh, and say, "Everyone, that's my mama, Mrs. Linda Monroe."

I direct everyone's attention to my mom. She turns around to show off her massive, bright yellow Aretha Franklin–style hat, with yellow, purple, and red flowers adorning any available space on, under, and around it. She curtsies and takes her seat again. There is joy in my heart that she's getting to witness me get married again, this time not for appearances or to follow a life script, but for love. And for inheriting another, albeit grown, granddaughter in Jabari's daughter.

"This is my bestie, Trevor. Don't mind him. He stays busy with the drama and hijinks. But if anyone here's looking for a husband, he'll make a good one."

"Thanks, Justin," Trevor says, taking his seat again.

"Well, seeing no objections," Lenay continues, "I'm pleased to introduce to you the happy husbands, Justin Monroe and Jabari Braxton. You may kiss your partner."

Jabari and I lean in and kiss like there's no audience of a hundred-plus friends and family watching. I feel his hand on the small of my back. Oh, his touch.

Jabari shifts to whisper in my ear, "I can't wait to get busy with you tonight, my love, and for the rest of our lives."

I wink and whisper back, "Busy ain't the half of it."

About the Authors

CHAZ LAMAR CRUZ was raised in the deserts and cities of Southern California by his Louisianan maternal grandmother. He is a graduate of Cal State LA and the University of San Francisco. Chaz is a poet, educator, and creative who writes from a place of possibility and wonder. He can be contacted at ChazLamar.com or Instagram/Twitter: @chzcruz.

Originally from Detroit, FREDERICK SMITH is a graduate of the Missouri School of Journalism, Loyola University Chicago, and Loyola Marymount University. He lives in San Francisco. He is author of *In Case You Forgot* (co-authored with Chaz Lamar Cruz), *Play It Forward*, *Right Side of the Wrong Bed*, and *Down For Whatever*.

He can be contacted at www.FrederickLSmith.com or Instagram/Twitter: @fsmith827.

Books Available From Bold Strokes Books

Busy Ain't the Half of It by Frederick Smith and Chaz Lamar Cruz. Elijah and Justin seek happily-ever-afters in LA, but are they too busy to notice happiness when it's there? (978-1-63555-944-6)

Pursuit: A Victorian Entertainment by Felice Picano. An intelligent, handsome, ruthlessly ambitious young man who rose from the slums to become the right-hand man of the Lord Exchequer of England will stop at nothing as he pursues his Lord's vanished wife across Continental Europe. (978-1-63555-870-8)

Best of the Wrong Reasons by Sander Santiago. For Fin Ness and Orion Starr, it takes a funeral to remind them that love is worth living for. (978-1-63555-867-8)

Coming to Life on South High by Lee Patton. Twenty-one-year-old gay virgin Gabe Rafferty's first adult decade unfolds as an unpredictable journey into sex, love, and livelihood. (978-1-63555-906-4)

Death's Prelude by David S. Pederson. In this prequel to the Detective Heath Barrington Mystery series, Heath discovers that first love changes you forever and drives you to become the person you're destined to be. (978-1-63555-786-2)

His Brother's Viscount by Stephanie Lake. Hector Somerville wants to rekindle his illicit love affair with Viscount Wentworth, but he must overcome one problem: Wentworth still loves Hector's brother. (978-1-63555-805-0)

The Dubious Gift of Dragon Blood by J. Marshall Freeman. One day Crispin is a lonely high school student—the next he is fighting a war in a land ruled by dragons, his otherworldly boyfriend at his side. (978-1-63555-725-1)

Quake City by St John Karp. Can Andre find his best friend Amy before the night devolves into a nightmare of broken hearts, malevolent drag queens, and spontaneous human combustion? Or has it always happened this way, every night, at Aunty Bob's Quake City Club? (978-1-63555-723-7)

Death Overdue by David S. Pederson. Did Heath turn to murder in an alcohol-induced haze to solve the problem of his blackmailer, or was it someone else who brought about a death overdue? (978-1-63555-711-4)

Every Summer Day by Lee Patton. Meant to celebrate every summer day, Luke's journal instead chronicles a love affair as fast-moving and possibly as fatal as his brother's brain tumor. (978-1-63555-706-0)

Everyday People by Louis Barr. When film star Diana Danning hires private eye Clint Steele to find her son, Clint turns to his former West Point barracks mate, and ex-buddy with benefits, Mars Hauser to lend his cyber espionage and digital black ops skills to the case.(978-1-63555-698-8)

Cirque des Freaks and Other Tales of Horror by Julian Lopez. Explore the pleasure of horror in this compilation that delivers like the horror classics…good ole tales of terror. (978-1-63555-689-6)

Royal Street Reveillon by Greg Herren. In this Scotty Bradley mystery, someone is killing the stars of a reality show, and it's up to Scotty Bradley and the boys to find out who. (978-1-63555-545-5)

Death Takes a Bow by David S. Pederson. Alan Keys takes part in a local stage production, but when the leading man is murdered, his partner Detective Heath Barrington is thrust into the limelight to find the killer. (978-1-63555-472-4)

Accidental Prophet by Bud Gundy. Days after his grandmother dies, Drew Morten learns his true identity and finds himself racing against time to save civilization from the apocalypse. (978-1-63555-452-6)

Counting for Thunder by Phillip Irwin Cooper. A struggling actor returns to the Deep South to manage a family crisis but finds love and ultimately his own voice as his mother is regaining hers for possibly the last time. (978-1-63555-450-2)

Of Echoes Born by 'Nathan Burgoine. A collection of queer fantasy short stories set in Canada from Lambda Literary Award finalist 'Nathan Burgoine. (978-1-63555-096-2)

CPSIA information can be obtained
at www.ICGtesting.com
Printed in the USA
LVHW091522090821
694908LV00005B/111